END OF HIS ROPE

Fargo heard a swishing and looked up as a lasso sailed from above and settled around him. Instantly it was yanked tight, pinning his arms to his sides. There was a loud whoop and the drumming of hooves, and he was dragged on his face through the dirt main street of Beartown.

But Cord's men weren't finished with him. The rider with the rope spurred his mount so that the rope whipped Fargo against a wagon with savage force.

For a brief moment the rope went slack. Before the rider could pull it taut, Fargo slipped out of the noose.

He was on his feet. He was bleeding, but his Colt was steady. Cord's riders had had their fun. Now it was the Trailsman's turn. . . .

BLAZING NEW TRAILS
WITH THE ACTION-PACKED
TRAILSMAN SERIES
BY JON SHARPE

☐	THE TRAILSMAN #115: GOLD MINE MADNESS	(169964—$3.50)
☐	THE TRAILSMAN #117: GUN VALLEY	(170482—$3.50)
☐	THE TRAILSMAN #118: ARIZONA SLAUGHTER	(170679—$3.50)
☐	THE TRAILSMAN #119: RENEGADE RIFLES	(170938—$3.50)
☐	THE TRAILSMAN #120: WYOMING MANHUNT	(171063—$3.50)
☐	THE TRAILSMAN #121: REDWOOD REVENGE	(171306—$3.50)
☐	THE TRAILSMAN #123: DESERT DEATH	(171993—$3.50)
☐	THE TRAILSMAN #124: COLORADO QUARRY	(172132—$3.50)
☐	THE TRAILSMAN #125: BLOOD PRAIRIE	(172388—$3.50)
☐	THE TRAILSMAN #126: COINS OF DEATH	(172604—$3.50)
☐	THE TRAILSMAN #127: NEVADA WARPATH	(173031—$3.50)
☐	THE TRAILSMAN #128: SNAKE RIVER BUTCHER	(173686—$3.50)

THE
TRAILSMAN

131

BEARTOWN
BLOODSHED

by

Jon Sharpe

A SIGNET BOOK

SIGNET
Published by the Penguin Group
Penguin Books USA Inc., 375 Hudson Street,
New York, New York 10014, U.S.A.
Penguin Books Ltd, 27 Wrights Lane,
London W8 5TZ, England
Penguin Books Australia Ltd, Ringwood,
Victoria, Australia
Penguin Books Canada Ltd, 10 Alcorn Avenue,
Toronto, Ontario, Canada M4V 3B2
Penguin Books (N.Z.) Ltd, 182-190 Wairau Road,
Auckland 10, New Zealand

Penguin Books Ltd, Registered Offices:
Harmondsworth, Middlesex, England

First published by Signet, an imprint of New American Library,
a division of Penguin Books USA Inc.

First Printing, November, 1992
10 9 8 7 6 5 4 3 2 1

The first chapter of this book previously appeared in *Montana Fire Smoke*,
the one hundred thirtieth volume in this series.

 REGISTERED TRADEMARK—MARCA REGISTRADA

Printed in the United States of America

The Trailsman

Beginnings . . . they bend the tree and they mark the man. Skye Fargo was born when he was eighteen. Terror was his midwife, vengeance his first cry. Killing spawned Skye Fargo, ruthless, cold-blooded murder. Out of the acrid smoke of gunpowder still hanging in the air, he rose, cried out a promise never forgotten.

The Trailsman they began to call him all across the West: searcher, scout, hunter, the man who could see where others only looked, his skills for hire but not his soul, the man who lived each day to the fullest, yet trailed each tomorrow. Skye Fargo, the Trailsman, the seeker who could take the wildness of a land and the wanting of a woman and make them his own.

1860—Beartown, where those who asked too many questions wound up six feet under . . .

1

The trouble started the moment the two lovely women appeared.

Skye Fargo had taken hold of the saddle horn and was about to swing onto his pinto stallion when he spied the pair of blond beauties hurrying down the dusty street in his general direction. The sight of them would have stopped any man in his tracks, not only because both had full figures, long golden tresses, and almost perfect facial features, but because they were identical twins, alike as two peas in a pod. Every single male in sight was staring at them but they paid absolutely no attention. They walked side by side, their gazes fixed straight ahead, indicating by their bearing and their walk that they were proper ladies and not fallen doves from any of the many saloons in Beartown. Their demeanor should have discouraged any of the rowdier element from bothering them.

But it didn't.

Fargo saw three men who had been lounging in front of The Lucky Dollar straighten and step farther out into the street, blocking the path of the women. The two lovelies both paused. In unison they frowned and went to bypass the men. But the youngest of the male trio, a dandy in a fine suit and a wide-brimmed white hat, grabbed the nearest woman by the wrist and held fast. She gave him a look that would have melted a rock, and when he made a comment, she tried to pull her arm free to no avail. All three men laughed.

Skye had seen enough. He let go of the saddle horn and walked toward the troublemakers. Oddly, none of the other men lining the street made any move to intervene and ordinarily western men wouldn't tolerate seeing a decent woman bothered. He loosened his big Colt in its holster and held his arm loose, ready for action. Neither the women nor the men, who had their backs to him, noticed him approach, and when he was close enough he heard the dandy speaking.

"—no call to be so unfriendly, Mercia. I just want you to have a drink with me, is all."

"You know darn well, Lucas Cord, that I don't drink," responded the woman whose arm he held. "Now let me go this instant or else."

"Or else what?" Lucas responded in a mocking tone. "You'll call the marshal?"

The other two men chuckled. Both wore typical frontier clothes and had pistols on their right hips. One was bearded, the other as thin as a rail.

"Leave my sister be!" threw in the second blonde, taking a half step toward Lucas Cord. "There are good men in this town who will hold you to account if you harm us."

"I don't want to harm you," Lucas replied, still holding Mercia's wrist. "All I want is a little company." He lowered his voice. "And as for the good men of Beartown, there isn't a damn one who will lift a finger against me and you know it."

By then Fargo was directly behind the dandy. "Wrong," he said, and seizing Cord by the shoulder he spun him partially around and planted a sweeping right fist on the point of Cord's angular chin. The man tottered backward, releasing Mercia in the process, and crashed onto his back. For several seconds no one else moved. They all appeared stunned. Then one of the other men, the bearded one, made a grab for the revolver strapped around his waist. Fargo palmed and leveled his Colt before the man could clear leather, and the bearded man froze. "Pull that and you'll be six feet under by sundown," he warned.

Blinking in disbelief, the bearded man slowly raised his gun hand. "Damn!" he exclaimed. "Never saw anyone that fast before."

Fargo wagged his Colt at the dazed Cord. "Pick up your friend and get out of here. And don't let me catch you bothering these ladies again."

The thin man, who wore a brown shirt, jeans, and a black hat, cocked his head to study Skye intently. "I don't know who you are, mister, but you're making a big mistake."

"I've made them before," Fargo said, "and I'm still alive. Now do as I told you before you make me lose my temper."

"Let's do as he says, Tillman," the bearded one declared nervously. He moved over to Lucas Cord and hooked his arm under one shoulder. After a moment's hesitation the man called Tillman took the other side and together they hoisted Cord erect and carted him off into the saloon.

Only then did Skye slip the Colt into his holster and tip his hat to the women. "Ladies," he said politely, and started to turn.

"Hold on!" Mercia exclaimed. "We must thank you for your gallant rescue. Who are you sir?"

"Skye Fargo."

"I'm Mercia Whitman and this is my sister, Marcia."

Close up, Skye still couldn't tell them apart. They both had striking green eyes and smooth complexions, their rosy mouths were exactly the same shape, and even their noses were identical. He'd seen twins before but never two so alike. "Please'd to meet you," he said. "Now if you'll excuse me," he added, and again went to leave.

"What's your hurry, Mr. Fargo?" Mercia asked, impulsively taking his arm.

"I'm on my way to Fort Laramie to see an old friend," Fargo explained.

"You don't intend to stay the night in Beartown?" Marcia inquired.

"No, ma'am," Skye answered. "I just stopped off to buy a few supplies and wet my whistle." He realized their voices were also identical and wondered how in the world anyone could tell the two apart.

Mercia and Marcia exchanged a strange glance and Marcia nodded.

"Surely you have time for some coffee?" Mercia then said. "Allow us to treat you. It's the least we can do for the service you've rendered."

Skye didn't feel particularly thirsty. But he wasn't about to pass up the chance to enjoy the company of two beautiful women. And since he had plenty of time to reach Fort Laramie, there was no reason to decline the invitation. "All right," he said. "Where to?"

"There's a nice restaurant just down the street," Marcia said.

"Lead the way," Fargo directed, and was pleasantly surprised when the sisters stepped up, one on each side of him, and hooked an arm in the crook of his elbow. They began walking and he fell into step. To a casual bystander it appeared as if he was doing the escorting.

"We'd like you to tell us all about yourself," Mercia commented.

"Oh, yes," Marcia confirmed. "Everything. It isn't often we meet a gentleman of your caliber."

Fargo grinned. He was certain they were up to something but for the life of him he couldn't figure out what it might be. Given the way they had acted toward Lucas Cord, they were being a bit too friendly, a bit too pushy. Not that he minded. He had been on the trail for days and relished this chance to enjoy the company of two such lovely women. Their perfume tingled his nostrils and he couldn't help but observe how nicely their bosoms filled out the tops of their attractive blue dresses. Which prompted a question. "I should think you ladies would wear different colored clothes just so folks can tell you apart."

They both giggled.

"We'll tell you a secret," Mercia said. "We *like* confusing people. Ever since we were babies no one has been able to tell which one of us was which except for our mother and father—." She broke off, sadness lining her face. Then she took a breath and continued. "It's been great fun. When we were younger we would change seats in school and our poor teacher would never know the difference."

"And we would pretend to be the other one at family gatherings and our relatives would never be the wiser," Marcia mentioned.

"How do your parents tell who is who?" Fargo idly asked.

"Our mother is dead," Mercia said softly. "She died on the way out here, over a year ago. Came down with a high fever one day after a rain and she never recovered. We didn't have a doctor on the wagon train so there was little we could do."

"Sorry to hear it," Fargo sympathized, and opted to

change the subject. "How about your father? How does he tell who is who?"

"We'll talk about him later," Mercia said.

"There's the restaurant," Marcia declared, pointing at an establishment bearing a large sign that read Ruth's Fine Eats. "Wait until you meet Ruth. She's the kindest person in this whole town."

Skye let himself be led to the double doors. Had he detected a trace of anger in Marcia's tone when she referred to the town or had it been his imagination? He opened a door for the sisters, then entered a spacious room containing four long tables lined with chairs. Red tablecloths and pink curtains gave the place a homey atmosphere, as did the delicious aroma of cooking food that wafted through an open door at the back of the room, through which the kitchen could be glimpsed. Only two other customers were there, an elderly couple in a corner.

Mercia moved to a table on the opposite side of the room and halted behind a chair.

"Allow me," Fargo said, and seated both of them before sitting with his back to the wall so he could keep an eye on the entrance. For all he knew, Lucas Cord might want revenge.

A white-haired matron in a lavender dress and a white apron came out of the kitchen, caught sight of them, and beamed as she walked on over. "Marcia and Mercia! How delightful. You girls haven't been in to see me in days."

"Hello, Ruth," Marcia responded. "We'd like some of your wonderful coffee."

"Sorry about not visiting you," Mercia said, and frowned. "But we've been too upset to go anywhere."

Ruth halted and nodded. "I understand, dearie." She glanced at Skye, examining him as she might an insect that had the temerity to trespass in her kitchen. "And who is this, might I ask?"

"His name is Skye Fargo," Mercia disclosed. "He just stopped Lucas Cord from giving us a bad time."

At the mention of Cord's name the matron's brown eyes narrowed. "Again?" she said absently, and wiped her thick hands on her apron. "When will that boy learn?"

"Lucas is no boy," Marcia said. "He's a lecher who thinks every woman should swoon at his feet when he smiles at them. One of these days he'll go too far and someone will put a bullet in his brain."

"For two cents I'd do it," Ruth said, and motioned at Marcia. "Why don't you join me in the kitchen for a minute. You can help me carry back the pot and cups."

"Certainly," Marcia replied.

Fargo watched them stroll off, then focused on Mercia, searching for a blemish, a mole perhaps or a tiny childhood scar that would enable him to tell the sisters apart. She steadily returned his stare and grinned.

"You're wasting your time, I assure you."

"Can you read thoughts?" Fargo joked.

"Experience, Mr. Fargo."

"Call me Skye," he said, and happened to turn toward the elderly couple in the corner. They were regarding him with the oddest expressions, and they immediately averted their gazes and forked roast beef into their mouths. Now what was that all about? he asked himself.

"Would you happen to be in need of money, Skye?" Mercia unexpectedly inquired.

Fargo looked at her. "The coffee will be thanks enough."

"I'm not offering to pay you for having helped us," Mercia said. "My sister and I are thinking of hiring you for a job we can't do ourselves."

"Oh? When did you decide this? I don't recollect the two of you talking about it on the way to the restaurant."

"We didn't have to discuss it," Mercia said. "This might seem bizarre to you, but frequently we know what the other is thinking without having to say a word. We've been this way since we were little girls." She paused. "I can still recall the very first time it happened. We were at the supper table and I wanted the butter. It was on the other side of Marcia, and before I could open my mouth to ask for it she handed the dish to me. I don't know what to call this talent but it definitely exists. Marcia and I are living proof."

"So you do read thoughts," Skye said, smiling. "Maybe the two of you should sign up with a traveling show. You could make good money."

Mercia laughed. "No thanks. I don't want to be considered a freak of nature. My sister and I don't advertise our talent. It's strictly between us, and even then we don't always see eye to eye. Although we're practically identical physically there are certain differences between us. Her personality is nothing like mine. She seldom loses her composure while I am very emotional."

Fargo was about to remark that he liked emotional women when the double doors slammed open and in strode an enraged Lucas Cord, a smirking Tillman, and the guy with the beard. Cord glared about until he spied Fargo, then he squared his shoulders and stalked forward. An ivory-handled Colt had been thrust in the waistband of his pants and his right hand hovered near it like the talons of a bird of prey about to swoop down on a rabbit or some such.

"You!" Cord bellowed. "On your feet! I don't like to kill a man who doesn't have a fair break."

Skye sighed and pushed his chair back from the table. For a man who didn't go out of his way to seek trouble he certainly found more than his share. He had no desire to gun down this dandy who acted about ten sizes too big for his britches, but he wasn't about to back down, either. "You don't know when to leave well enough alone, Cord."

Lucas stopped, his body rigid. "You hit me, you son of a bitch! Now stand up and take your medicine."

Whether it was Cord's insolent tone or the fact these men were prodding him when all he wanted was to be left alone, Fargo couldn't say. But suddenly something snapped deep inside of him and he came out of his chair so swiftly that Lucas Cord involuntarily took a step backward and Tillman lost his arrogant smirk. Instead of drawing, Fargo walked straight toward them. The guy with the beard look as if he desperately wanted to be somewhere else. Tillman seemed startled. And Cord's right hand trembled above his gun.

"That's close enough!" Lucas cried, extending his left hand, palm out. "Stop right there."

Skye had no intention of stopping. He advanced until he was mere inches from Cord and snapped, "Go ahead. Die if you want to."

Lucas Cord gulped. His face became a bright shade of crimson. He clenched and unclenched his right hand, then abruptly moved a pace backward and crouched like a cougar about to pounce. "You don't know who you're dealing with, mister," he growled. "I'm the son of Rory Cord."

"So?"

Surprise etched Cord's face. "Rory Cord, owner of the RC ranch," he elaborated in a tone that implied his father was a man to be reckoned with.

"Never heard of it."

"Everyone has heard of my father," Lucas said in disbelief, then added smugly, "He's the biggest man in these parts. And when you tangle with me, you tangle with him."

Contempt welled up in Fargo. Here was a grown man of twenty or so hiding behind his father's shirttails. Lucas expected him to be intimidated by the news and to back down. Lucas was sadly mistaken. "This is between you and me," he stated flatly. "Your father isn't the one who bothered these women. You did. And now you have the gall to march in here and threaten me. Boy, you're as dumb as they come."

"I'm no boy!" Lucas bristled, and without warning lunged, swinging both fists at Skye's head.

Taken unawares, Fargo was rocked by a right to the jaw. Backpedaling, he brought his arms up to protect his face and stomach and warded off several wild punches. Cord seemed to have forgotten all about the gun in his waistband in his mad fury to smash Skye to a pulp. But reckless rage was a poor substitute for seasoned skill, and Fargo had lived through more fights and wild brawls than most ten men. He blocked a blow to the abdomen, then landed a looping right full on Cord's mouth, smashing Cord's lips and sending the dandy staggering into a table. Before Lucas could recover Fargo closed in. He rammed his knuckles into Cord's mouth again as Lucas tried to straighten, then delivered a flurry that battered Cord to his knees. Nearly senseless, Cord swayed. Fargo set himself for one final blow when a sharp cry of warning from Mercia rent the air.

"Skye! Behind you!"

Fargo whirled to behold Tillman armed with a dagger just as the thin man sprang.

2

Skye Fargo had honed his reflexes on the rugged frontier where danger lurked behind every bend in the trail. The difference between life and death often depended on a fraction of an instant of reaction time. Sometimes all the warning a man had was the buzz of an arrow through the air or the scrape of claws on a boulder as a mountain lion attacked. Men who were slow were men who died. The best frontiersmen and the warriors who counted the most coup were those who possessed the instincts of the wild creatures they frequently fought, and Skye Fargo was widely acknowledged as the best of the best.

So even as Tillman charged and lanced his gleaming dagger at Skye's chest, Skye was pivoting on the heel of his right foot and sliding sideways. The blade missed his buckskins by a hair. He clamped both hands on Tillman's outstretched arm, twisted, and heaved.

The thin man sailed a half-dozen feet onto a chair, shattering it as he crashed to the floor.

Skye was there before Tillman could stand. Groggy and unsteady, Tillman got to one knee, weakly waving his dagger. Skye swept his right boot up, hitting the man flush on the jaw, and Tillman toppled. Taking a step, Skye was ready to wade in again but the thin man was out cold. He suddenly remembered the bearded man and spun, his hand swooping to his Colt.

"No, sir!" the man shouted, holding both hands out to show they were empty. He hadn't moved during the fight and made no attempt to do so now. "This was their doing, mister. I didn't want to tackle you again. You've made a believer out of me, whoever the hell you are."

Fargo glanced around. Ruth and Marcia had come from the kitchen and were standing near Mercia.

"Allow me to introduce you," Ruth said to the

bearded man. "Grundel, this is Skye Fargo. Mr. Fargo, Grundel is one of Rory Cord's hands."

Grundel's blood appeared to drain from his face. "Skye Fargo?" he blurted, and licked his thick lips. "Did you say Skye Fargo?"

"That's my handle," Fargo confirmed. "What of it?"

"Nothing. Nothing at all," Grundel said, shaking his head vigorously. "I don't want no trouble with you, Mr. Fargo, sir. Hell, I've been hearing stories about you for years. Only a jackass would buck you." He must have remembered trying to draw on Skye earlier because his features went blank and he blanched even more. "Sweet Jesus, I nearly got myself killed!"

"Drag these two out of here," Fargo ordered. "And tell them that if they buck me again, I won't go easy on them."

"Yes, sir. I surely will. But I feel it's only right to warn you that Rory Cord will be fit to be tied when he hears about this. He'll come after you, Mr. Fargo, sir, and he won't be alone."

"Let him come," Fargo growled.

"Yes, sir," Grundel said, and moved over to Lucas who was still on his knees with his eyes closed and his arms drooping. He took hold of Cord from behind and began dragging him from the restaurant.

"Sorry about the chair," Fargo said to Ruth. "I'll pay for it if you want."

"No need," she responded, grinning. "It was worth it to see Lucas and Tillman get their due. I only wish it had been Rory Cord instead of his son."

"I take it they throw their weight around a lot."

"You don't know the half of it," Ruth said, and gestured at the coffeepot and cups on the table. "Why don't you sit a spell and let us bend your ear. The girls want to make you a proposition. They need help bad and I've told Marcia they couldn't find a better man anywhere than you."

Skye stepped to the table and sat down, his blood still racing in his veins. His brief stay in Bear River City, or Beartown as the locals referred to it, was turning into more than he bargained for. All he'd wanted were a few things he couldn't rustle up for himself—coffee, salt, and flour. In the bargain he had rustled up an impending

18

confrontation with a man he knew nothing about. "Tell me about Rory Cord."

The twins sat while Ruth poured coffee for all of them, talking as she worked. "Rory Cord hails from back East, from New York some say. He showed up in Beartown about two years ago and started throwing money around like he was King Midas. Had a huge house and barn built north of town about ten miles and then had five hundred head of cattle brought in from down in Texas. He fancies the notion of setting himself up like one of those big Texas cattle barons."

Fargo nodded knowingly, then took a sip of the piping hot coffee. Once the vast territory stretching from Fort Laramie to the Bear River had been home to only Indians and the buffalo, a region hordes of settlers passed through as they wound along the Oregon Trail but which none had bothered to homestead. In recent years a few hardy towns like Beartown had sprung up and there were more and more men like Rory Cord moving in with grand plans to establish ranching empires. One day, the newspapers claimed, the territory would rival Texas in the number of cattle sent to the waiting markets in the East.

"Cord brought in eight or nine hands," Ruth was saying. "At first everything was fine. Cord was a high and mighty so-and-so, but he didn't bother anyone much." She put down the pot, then looked at the entrance as Grundel came back in for Tillman. "It wasn't until his son joined him that all hell broke loose. Lucas thinks he's the cock of the roost and walks over everyone. He bullies folks into getting his own way and has no regard for anyone's feelings other than his own."

Fargo heard Mercia utter an unladylike snort. Or was it Marcia? They were no longer seated in the same chairs as before and he had lost track of which one was which.

"Lucas also thinks every single woman in town should vie for the honor of wiping his boots clean," Mercia said angrily. "You saw for yourself out in the street. He can't keep his hands off of us, and when we object he gets nasty."

"Most of the men in town are afraid of him," Marcia added. "Or of his father, I should say. They know if they lay a hand on Lucas that Rory will come after them."

"Gives me something to look forward to," Fargo said, and swallowed more coffee.

Ruth settled into a chair across from him. "All of this ties in with what the girls are about to ask you. I hope you'll hear them out before you answer."

"I'm listening."

Mercia—or was it Marcia?—cleared her throat. "Skye, our father is Adam Whitman. Until a week ago he ran the town newspaper and he took his work very seriously." She gazed wistfully out the nearest window. "Originally, he intended to travel to Oregon and start a paper out there. He's been a journalist for twenty years and you might say the work is in his blood."

"But when Mother died he was devastated." The other sister took over the narrative. "We reached Beartown and that was as far as he cared to go. So we've been here ever since."

"And neither of us like it," Mercia resumed. "We've made do, and although Papa keeps insisting we should go back East and live with his sister and her family we're not about to leave him all alone. He's been a wonderful father to us and we owe him that."

Fargo was impressed with their devotion and remarked as much.

"We love our father," Marcia—or was it Merica?— said. "And now he's disappeared and we have nowhere to turn."

"Disappeared?"

Both sisters nodded.

"A week ago he rode out to the north," Mercia said. "He wouldn't tell us where he was going, only that he expected to be back by supper." She bowed her head. "He never did return."

The other twin went on. "For some time before that he had been acting very secretive. Two or three times he rode off late at night and didn't come home until morning. When we asked him, all he would say was that he was investigating a matter he must keep confidential for the time being. Then he ups and vanishes without a trace. We believe there's a connection and we need someone to find out what happened."

Marcia and Mercia stared at him.

"So you want me to take the job." Fargo deduced the

obvious, and lifted the coffee cup to his lips to buy some time to think. As much as he liked the twins, and he was strongly attracted to both of them, he wasn't too keen on the idea of spending countless hours in the saddle scouring the countryside for Adam Whitman when he was supposed to be on his way to Fort Laramie. Given their story, Whitman might indeed have met with foul play. But it was equally as likely that an accident had befallen the man. Lone riders often fell prey to roving war parties or were stranded when their mounts suffered a broken leg and succumbed to the elements or hunger and thirst. "Isn't there a marshal in Beartown? This sounds like a job for him."

"There's Fred Bullock, but he's not much of a marshal," Marcia replied. "He spends all his time hanging around the saloons and stuffing his face with food."

Mercia nodded. "We went to him when our father failed to come home and he organized a search party. They were gone for a day and a half and came back empty-handed. They didn't even find Papa's horse."

"We've written to the army and the closest federal marshal," Marcia continued, "but you know how it is. It might be weeks or months before we hear from either."

Again Fargo nodded. The army had its hands full with the Indians and could seldom afford to devote precious time and resources to a single missing civilian. And the federal marshals were too few and too busy tracking down known killers and other criminals to involve themselves in a hunt for a missing person. "I can see your problem," he admitted.

Mercia leaned toward him. "Will you help us then? We're not rich by any means, but we can pay you three hundred dollars if you'll find our father."

"Even if I agree, there's no guarantee I'll find him," Fargo pointed out. "I hate to be blunt, but if his horse went down and he couldn't locate water or food then his bones might be lying out on the prairie or somewhere in the mountains."

Both twins stiffened.

"We're aware of that," Mercia said.

"But we have to know," Marcia stated. "How would you feel if it was your father?"

Ruth coughed to get their attention. "There's something you girls should be thinking on. If Fargo leaves Beartown right this minute, odds are he'll be long gone before Rory Cord shows up. But if he stays to help you, then as sure as you're sitting there he'll have to face Rory and Rory's outfit and you both know what that means."

Fargo placed his cup on the table. The silent appeal in the eyes of the twins touched him deeply, but he was loath to waste his time and their money on a possibly fruitless search. He opened his mouth to stress that point when the front door slammed.

Into the restaurant waddled a heavyset man whose baggy clothes only added to the impression he gave of immense bulk. Weighing three hundred pounds or better, he moved ponderously, breathing heavily with each stride. On his left hip was a Colt. Pinned to his brown vest was a tarnished silver badge. He came up to their table and hooked his pudgy thumbs in his gunbelt. "I'm Fred Bullock, marshal here," he announced, gazing at Skye. "I've just learned that you've been giving Lucas Cord a hard time. We don't like strangers coming into this town and beating up decent citizens, mister."

Ruth laughed. "Lucas Cord a decent citizen? Have you been hitting the bottle hard today, Fred?"

Bullock shot her a spiteful glance. "This doesn't concern you, Miss Heatherton. Kindly mind your own affairs."

"Why certainly, Marshal," Ruth said demurely. "But I'm curious. Have you been talking to Lucas about this man?"

"No," Bullock answered. "Lucas is at the doctor's being patched up. He's unconscious. But Grundel told me this hombre stomped Lucas and Tillman, both."

"Did Grundel tell you who this man is?" Ruth asked.

"No. I saw Grundel and a few other men lugging Cord and Tillman into the doc's so I went over to see what was going on. Grundel told me they'd tangled with a stranger at your place and described the stranger. He never mentioned a name," Bullock said. "What difference does it make?"

"Grundel never did like you much," Ruth said.

"So? I don't care one way or the other who likes me and who doesn't. As for Grundel, he's nothing but a dumb two-bit cowhand who gets up every day on the wrong side of the bed."

"Maybe he's not as dumb as you think," Ruth stated.

The marshal impatiently hitched up his gunbelt. "What the dickens are you getting at, Miss Heatherton? I have work to do and can't be listening to you babble on like an old biddy hen."

Ruth's features clouded over. "My apologies, Marshal Bullock. I certainly don't want to waste your time." She smiled sweetly. "Allow me to introduce Skye Fargo."

"Fargo?" Bullock said, his brow creasing. "Why is that name familiar? I know I've heard it somewhere."

"I would imagine you have," Ruth said. "Most folks call him the Trailsman. They say he's killed more men than Kit Carson and can read sign better than Daniel Boone."

Fred Bullock took a step back and slowly lowered his hands so they were nowhere near his revolver. "I recollect some of the stories now," he said, and began gnawing on his fleshy lower lip.

Skye raised his coffee cup to his mouth to hide his spreading grin. Sometimes, he reflected, having a widespread reputation came in handy. Ordinarily he shunned notoriety, but in an instance like this where he could use his fame to avoid needless bloodshed, he welcomed it. Because there was no way he would let himself be bullied or prodded when he had done nothing wrong, and if the marshal pushed too hard he would push right back.

Bullock took a ridiculously long time to mull over what he would do. At length he sniffed and said, "Well, Trailsman or not I can't let you ride on into Beartown and cause a ruckus. Not unless you have a damn good reason. Let me hear your side of the story."

Mercia answered before Skye. "He came to our aid when Lucas manhandled me."

"You know how Lucas is," Marcia said. "So leave this poor man alone and go bother someone else."

The marshal was unruffled. "You have no call to talk to me like that, missy," he said calmly. Then he nodded at Fargo. "I reckon I'll let it go, this time. But I don't want to hear of you stirring things up again. Savvy?"

"Tell that to Lucas Cord," Skye responded testily.

"I will," Bullock said, and began to leave. He stopped

after taking a couple of paces and looked over his sloping shoulder. "How long do you figure on being in town?"

"As long as I want to be," Skye said.

Bullock sighed. "I was afraid you'd say that." He strolled out, slamming the door behind him.

"I never will understand why he was picked to be town marshal," Marcia commented in the ensuing silence.

"Fred was picked because no one else wanted the job," Ruth said. "And don't take him lightly. He's not very fast with a gun and he isn't a fast thinker, but he's basically an honest man and he's had enough backbone to buck Rory Cord on occasion."

Fargo's estimation of the marshal rose a few notches. Most small town lawmen would shy away from bucking the richest and most powerful man in their territory. In some towns the marshal or sheriff was no better than a puppet, doing whatever the vested interests demanded in order to keep his job. If Fred Bullock had been standing up to the Cords then the man was a better lawman than he appeared at first glance.

"Forget about him. We have something far more important to discuss," Mercia said. She reached over to gently rest her warm palm on the top of Skye's right hand. "What about our problem? Will you help us?"

Marcia clasped Skye's other hand in her own. "Please say you'll try to find our father. You're our last hope. By the time we hear from the army or a federal marshal the trail will be cold." She lightly ran a fingernail along his wrist. "Don't make us beg."

Fargo disliked being put on the spot. His natural inclination was to decline. But having those four beautiful eyes bore into him in hopeful expectation was more than any man could endure. And their faces, so delightfully smooth and radiating sensual vitality, shattered his resolve. He found himself musing on what it would be like to make love to one of them and his manhood twitched at the prospect.

"Please," Mercia pleaded.

"All right," Fargo replied, frowning in annoyance at his capitulation. "I'll see what I can do. But I'm not making any promises and I can't stick around here more than a few days."

Both twins squealed happily and clapped their hands. Ruth smiled and nodded.

"If there is anything we can do, just say so," Marcia said.

At least Skye thought it was Marcia but he wasn't completely sure. He glanced from one to the other, deciding they both had mouths like ripe cherries. "There must be a clue somewhere as to what your father was up to. Did you go through all of his effects?"

"We went through everything," Mercia answered. "His desk, his file cabinet, his records at home. We checked all the letters he'd saved and we even went through all the pockets in his clothes." She shook her head. "Nothing."

"We also asked around, going to friends of the family and acquaintances here in Beartown," Marcia mentioned. "No one knew a thing. We were at our wit's end until we bumped into you."

Fargo pondered different angles before asking, "You say he rode out of town to the north. Was he using his own horse or did he rent one?"

"He had his own. We all do, and we board them at the livery at the west end of the street," Mercia said. "His was a fine bay."

"What kind of temperament did it have?"

"It was as tame as could be, it that's what you're getting at," Mercia said. "He had if for four years and rode it everywhere. Never once did I hear of it shying or being spooked by a snake or a rabbit or whatnot. A child could have ridden it without any problem."

Fargo shoved to his feet. The sooner he began, the sooner he would be on his way to Fort Laramie. Although it seemed pointless, his only recourse was to do some asking around on his own. "I guess I'll get started."

"Are you fixing to ride out of town?" Mercia inquired.

"No," Fargo said. "It's too late in the day for that. Tomorrow morning I'll head out and make a sweep north of Beartown to see if I can find any week-old tracks. It's a long shot but you never know."

"Where will you spend the night?" Marcia wanted to know.

"Is there a hotel here?"

The twins shared fleeting looks.

"We wouldn't hear of you spending money to stay alone in a cramped hotel room," Mercia said. "There's a spare bedroom at our house and your welcome to spend the night with us."

"What will people think?" Ruth broke in.

"We don't care," Marcia told her. "We're grown women and can do as we please, thank you very much."

"What do you say?" Mercia addressed Skye. "The spare bedroom is on the ground floor and our bedrooms are upstairs so you'll have all the privacy you could want and won't bother us in the least."

Fargo had to stare out a window as if contemplating his decision so they wouldn't note the twinkle in his eyes. He already had his mind made up. While a perfect gentleman would decline their courteous offer, he had never claimed to be perfect. And the idea of sharing the same house with them aroused a hunger that had nothing to do with food. If he was incredibly lucky he might get to satisfy his appetite. "You've convinced me. I'll stay with you."

"Thank you," Mercia said. "You won't regret it. We'll do our best to make your stay as pleasant as we can."

With a straight face Fargo said, "I'm counting on it."

3

Skye's first stop was the livery stable. Leading the Ovaro, he walked down the main street, aware of the many stares cast in his direction by the good citizens of Beartown, and halted near the wide open doors. Word of his fight with Lucas Cord must have already spread, which was typical of small towns where the most exciting topic of daily conversation was the weather. He spied a brawny man in coveralls forking hay into a stall at the rear of the stable. "Howdy," he called, entering. "Need to put up my horse for a spell."

The liveryman jerked his pitchfork at an empty stall. "Put 'im there. Hay is free but oats are extra and you do your own grooming."

"Fine with me," Fargo said, bringing the Ovaro up the aisle. "Your name is Kellerman, isn't it?"

The pitchfork paused above the mound of hay and the liveryman shifted to coldly scrutinize Skye. "What if it is, stranger?"

"Mercia and Marcia Whitman tell me their father boarded his horse with you. Were you here the day he rode off and never came back?"

Kellerman lowered the pitchfork and jabbed the sharp metal prongs into the ground. "Maybe I was. Maybe I wasn't. I'm a man who likes to mind his own business."

"So do I most of the time," Fargo said, stopping a few feet away. "But the ladies have asked me to find out what happened to their father and I aim to oblige them."

"Sometimes it's not healthy to poke your nose in where it doesn't belong, stranger," Kellerman said.

"Is this one of those times?"

"Could be," Kellerman responded, shrugging. "Either way it's none of my business. All I care about is my business and my family. Do you have a family, mister?"

"No. Not yet."

Kellerman yanked the pitchfork loose. "When you do, you'll change your tune. You'll keep your nose to the grindstone and won't get involved in the affairs of others." He speared the fork into the hay. "Healthier that way." Spinning on his heels, he walked out the back door.

Skye took the stallion into the empty stall. Was there more to the liveryman's words than seemed apparent? Did Kellerman know something? Had that been a friendly warning? He stripped his gear and saddle off the pinto and gave it a rubdown using handfuls of crushed straw. Then he fed it a heaping pile of fresh hay with the pitchfork, draped his saddle and bedroll over the side of the stall, and grabbed his saddlebags and Sharps rifle on his way back out to the street.

In another hour it would be dark. The twins had offered to cook for him so he strolled toward their house, situated almost directly across from the restaurant. A score of townspeople were outside and a handful of men stood in front of one of the saloons. Two boys were playing fetch with a mongrel across the way, the dog yipping crazily until one or the other threw the stick.

It was uncanny, Fargo thought, how much small western towns were alike. All had the same dusty streets, the same flimsy frame buildings sporting false fronts with oversized painted signs. There was always at least one stable, a general store, and an eatery. Plus as many saloons as the male population could profitably support. To a man like himself, accustomed to the wide open spaces, to the limitless plains and the majestic mountains, towns and cities were too confining for comfort. Sometimes, as he walked along a narrow street with buildings rearing on either side, he had the impression he was in an immense wooden cage and he longed for the wild lands he loved so much. He felt that way now as he passed the mouth of an alley. And preoccupied as he was, he didn't detect the flicker of motion in the depths of the alley until it was too late.

Skye heard a swishing noise and looked up as a rope sailed from above and settled around him. Instantly it was yanked tight, the loop constricting around his elbows and waist, pinning his arms at his sides. There was a loud whoop and the drumming of hoofs and he glanced into the alley to see a horse and rider bearing down on him at a full gallop. He tried to leap clear but the horse was on him in a flash, pain flaring in his shoulder as the animal rammed into him and sent him sprawling in the dust. His forehead hit hard and he lost his grip on the Sharps and the saddlebags.

Wicked laughter cut the air.

Fargo tried to rise to his knees and went to flex his arms to cast off the rope. But suddenly it was pulled taut and he was violently yanked onto his back, torment racking his spine, to hurtle along the ground like a stone skimming a pond. The rider was going to drag him down the street! He grimaced and thrashed, trying to break free, but the rope was like wire and he couldn't get the leverage he needed to apply his full strength. His hat flew off. His left leg hit hard and went numb. Then, as quickly as he had lurched into motion, he rolled to a stop.

More laughter mocked him.

He lifted his head, spit bitter dust from his mouth, and saw two riders nearby. Both wore clothes typical of cowhands. They cackled and pointed at him.

"One more time, Burt?" the one with the lariat looped around his saddle horn asked his friend.

Burt nodded. "Teach the son of a bitch a lesson, Clem."

Skye lunged to his feet, his right hand almost closing on the Colt. A heartbeat later the rider named Clem broke into a gallop again, coming straight at him, forcing him to jump awkwardly aside and giving him no time to draw before the rope tightened once more and he was hurled to the ground with bone-jarring force. He bounced and flopped like a rag doll at the end of a string, totally helpless. Inwardly, a wave of fury washed over him. He didn't need to be a genius to figure out these were some of Rory Cord's men intent on paying him back for what he had done to Lucas and Tillman.

Clem whooped again and angled toward the right side of the street.

Fargo was only vaguely aware of the gaping citizens lining the street, none of whom were likely to intervene on his behalf. For one thing, none of them knew him personally. For another, the two cowhands worked for Rory Cord and bucking them might arouse Cord's wrath. And since there was no telling where the marshal was or if Bullock would interfere, he was wholly on his own. Which was just the way he liked it.

He twisted his head to see Clem better and discovered the reason the young cowhand had altered his course. Parked in front of a boardwalk near the general store was a buckboard. Clem was making straight for it. He bunched his muscles and strived to tear the rope off but was unable to budge the loop. The cowhand, almost to the rig, suddenly reined to the left and gouged his spurs into his steed. Like an oversized whip the rope was flicked to the right in a sharp loop and Skye saw the buckboard loom before him. Clem had turned at just the right angle to send him crashing into it.

Skye resorted to pure reflex. He rolled to the left, or tried to, and almost cried out when his back slammed into a wheel. His left hand closed on a spoke and for a second he hung there as Clem sped on down the street and the slack rope became taut once more. In desperation he surged against the loop and felt it loosen slightly, enough so that when all the slack was taken up and the rope went rigid the momentum yanked the loop over and off his body.

He was loose! Pushing to his knees, he drew the Colt. Twenty yards away Clem woke up the fact the noose was empty, and he halted in a spray of dust. The cowhand wheeled his mount, spotted Skye, and rashly clawed for his gun.

"Don't!" someone cried.

Fargo banged off two shots. The slugs lifted Clem from his saddle and he plummeted to the ground with a thud. Whirling, Fargo saw the other cowhand a dozen yards off. Burt threw his empty hands skyward.

"No, sir! I don't want no part of gunplay!"

"Then don't so much as twitch," Fargo warned as he stood, training the Colt on the rider's chest. His shoulders and arms ached terribly but the worst discomfort was a throbbing pain in his right shoulder blade. He advanced warily.

"It wasn't supposed to come to this," Burt said, glancing sadly at his dead companion. "We wanted to have some fun at your expense, was all."

"Why?"

"We heard about Lucas and you. Figured we'd teach you to leave the Cords alone."

"I could have been killed," Fargo said, stopping and cocking the .44.

Burt gulped and shook his head. "Now you hold on there, mister! My pistol is in my holster. If you shoot me it will be murder, plain and simple."

"And what would you have called my death?" Fargo asked harshly. "An accident?" He was mad enough to squeeze the trigger at the slightest provocation but Burt had enough sense not to give him cause.

Heavy footsteps approached from the rear.

Fargo pivoted so he could keep an eye on the cowhand and make certain no one shot him in the back. The newcomer was none other than an extremely displeased Marshal Fred Bullock. "About time you showed up," Fargo remarked.

The huge man halted and glowered at Skye, then at Burt, then at the body sprawled in the middle of the street. "I knew you'd be trouble. I just knew it."

"They started it," Fargo said.

Bullock wiped the back of a pudgy hand across his brow and nodded. "I know. I heard a commotion and looked out my window as Clem tried to ride you into the buckboard. He was a hothead, forever getting into scrapes of one kind or another. This time he picked the wrong person to ride herd on."

Burt called out, "This wasn't my idea, Marshal. Clem had the notion and he was the one who lassoed the stranger. I didn't do a thing that you can arrest me for."

"Care to bet?" Bullock retorted, facing the cowhand. "I could haul you in right this minute for creating a disturbance." He stepped closer. "Too bad there isn't a law against being stupid or I'd haul you in for that, too."

"Then I'm free to go?" Burt asked hopefully.

"I'm not about to give you free room and board at the town's expense just because you're a jackass," Bullock responded, turning to Skye. "Unless, of course, you care to file charges against him. But I doubt a jury would convict him for having a part in this."

Fargo twirled the Colt into his holster. "You're right. It would be pointless. I won't file charges."

"You can go," Bullock told the cowhand. "But you tell your boss that I don't want any more shooting in Beartown or the culprit will answer to me."

"I'll tell him," Burt promised. He turned his horse, and raced off.

There were over two dozen people in the street now, most eager to get a good look at the slain cowhand. They ringed Clem's corpse, jostling for a better view.

Bullock watched them for a bit. "Lousy pack of vultures," he said, and looked at Fargo. "I don't suppose you plan to leave any time soon?"

"Not until I find out what happened to Adam Whitman."

"So that's why you were with the twins? Damn. I knew they wouldn't leave well enough alone."

"What can you tell me about his disappearance? I know you took out a search party and didn't turn up a thing," Skye said.

"But not from lack of trying," Bullock said. "We rode as far north as Cord ranch. Then we swept east and west as far as we thought practical, scouring every trail and checking every water hole." He frowned. "All we got for our effort was saddlesore."

"Was there any particular reason you headed for the Cord spread first?"

"Two reasons. Whitman was last seen riding north out of town. And it was common knowledge that Cord and Whitman hated each other. Whitman had written a few editorials in his paper criticizing Rory for allowing his men to get out of hand and Cord didn't appreciate them." Bullock paused. "Rory Cord is a vain bastard who acts as if he's some sort of king from one of those European countries, but I couldn't see him killing Whitman over something so trivial."

"You never know," Fargo remarked, and headed up the street to retrieve his hat, rifle, and saddlebags. "If you need to see me later I'll be at the Whitman's."

"If I was you I'd keep one eye over my shoulder at all times."

"Always," Fargo said. He had to admit that Bullock impressed him as being sincere. So maybe he had an ally in his hunt for the truth, but he had no way of knowing how far Bullock would back him up when Rory Cord finally showed up. And there was no doubt that Cord would be as mad as a rabid wolf over the beating his son had taken. Now Clem's death would add fuel to the fire.

He reclaimed his hat first, then found the Sharps and his saddlebags and made for the Whitman residence, ignoring the stares and the fingers pointing his way. Four men, under Bullock's direction, were carting the slain cowhand into the town jail, a small wood building with iron bars in all the windows.

The door to the house stood ajar and from within emanated strange clanking noises unlike any he had ever heard. Puzzled, he touched his thumb to the rifle hammer and his finger to the trigger, then gave the door a slight shove with the end of the barrel. He saw a desk and a potbellied stove, and over in the corner was either Mercia or Marcia hard at work on an unusual contraption that gave off the clanking sounds. "Hello," he greeted her, but she didn't hear him over the noise.

Fargo entered and crossed to the desk where he deposited his belongings. The twin had her dress sleeves rolled up and was pumping a heavy lever up and down with one hand while feeding a large sheet of paper into the metal machine with her other. He gazed at a framed newspaper on the wall, the very first edition of *The Beartown Chronicle*, and realized the front room of the house had served as Adam Whitman's office. When he looked at the twin she was looking at him and had stopped her work.

"Skye! I didn't hear you come in."

"Don't let me interrupt," Fargo said, leaning against the desk.

"I can use a break," she responded. "This old handpress is difficult to operate. After half an hour or so I always need a rest. Father, though, could work for six to eight hours without ever tiring."

"Are you putting out a newspaper?"

She nodded. "We're trying to keep the paper running but I don't know if we can do it all by ourselves. Marcia is out right now trying to collect from our advertisers. She won't be back for an hour or more."

So this was Mercia, Fargo noted, and grinned at the

33

ink smudges on her forearms, chin, and cheeks. "You really get into your work, don't you?"

"What?" she rejoined, moving to the mirror. "Oh, my," she gasped, then laughed gaily. "I'm certainly a sight."

"For sore eyes," Fargo said. "If you don't mind my saying so, both your sister and you are two of the best-looking women in this whole territory."

"Why would I mind?" Mercia asked, grinning impishly. She strolled over until she was standing right in front of him. "Only women who aren't comfortable with their femininity become upset when a man compliments them." Her grin widened. "Myself, I like a man who isn't afraid to—." Suddenly she broke off and examined the front of his buckskins. "Wait a minute. What on earth happened to you? Your clothes are all dirty and there's a tear in your pant leg."

"Didn't you hear the shots?"

Mercia nodded at the handpress. "With that antique operating I wouldn't hear the end of the world. Someone shot at you?"

"One of Cord's men tried to. I was a shade faster."

"Did you kill him?"

Fargo nodded.

"Rory Cord will be out for your blood now."

"I'll be ready."

Mercia went to the front door and closed it. "Come with me. I need to get this ink off and you can tidy up." She walked past him into a narrow hallway and moved along it to an open door. "This is where you'll sleep."

Inside was a bed, a chair, and a dresser. He put the Sharps and his saddlebags on the bed and rejoined her.

"This way," Mercia said, continuing along the hall to another door. This one admitted them to a small room containing a washbasin on a counter, a bar of lye soap nearby, and a folded towel and washcloth hanging on separate pegs. "Do you want to go first?"

"You can," Skye answered. He had admired the way her hips swayed suggestively as they moved down the hallway, and now he leaned on the jamb and let his eyes drink in the sensual contours of her ripe body as she removed the ink stains from her arms and face. Outside the sun was close to setting and in the house the light had dimmed, yet her hair glistened as if bathed in the radiance of direct sunlight.

Mercia finished washing and applied the towel to her face. "You certainly aren't shy, are you?" she asked, her back still to him.

"What do you mean?" Fargo responded.

"The way you keep looking at me, as if you haven't been near a woman in ages."

"Now how—?" Fargo began, taking a short step to the right. Then he understood. Between the washbasin and the wall was propped a small mirror and she had seen him eyeing her shape. "No, I'm not," he said bluntly. "When I see something I like, I don't make a secret of it."

"What a happy coincidence," Mercia said, dropping the towel on the counter. "Neither do I." She swung around, smiling enigmatically, and sashayed up to him. Her bosom was less than an inch from his broad chest, her eyes sparkling with a hint of a challenge. "I took a liking to you the moment I saw you."

"Lucky me."

"In more ways than you know."

Mercia abruptly pressed flush against him, boldy meeting his hungry gaze, and draped her slender arms over his shoulders. "As I said before, my sister won't be back for some time. We're all alone. Care to take advantage of the situation?"

He let his mouth do his talking by swooping his lips to hers and sliding his tongue into her mouth. She tasted of mint and her skin gave off a delicious raspberry scent, the lingering fragrance of her perfume. His hand traveled the length of her spine to rest on the curve of her hips. Her body gave off an animal heat that kindled the flames of his own passion. She had claimed to be the emotional one and she proved it now by transforming into a lust-filled Venus. Greedily, she sucked on his tongue and kissed his chin and neck. Her hands executed small circles all down his front until they hovered above his manhood.

Mercia broke off and leaned back. "Nice, big man. Very nice. You were an excellent choice if I do say so myself."

"I thought I was hired for my tracking ability," Fargo mentioned.

"You were," Mercia said. "But that wasn't all. My sister and I needed someone brave and dependable, and you fit the bill." She puckered and playfully blew him a kiss. "And it doesn't hurt that you're about as handsome as they come. Just looking at you gets me all excited."

"You should have told me sooner."

"In front of dear, sweet Ruth? She believes that Marcia and I are as prim and proper as they come. Little does she know we're both starved for a decent man. Most of the townsmen are married or have as much appeal as bumps on logs. Some of the cowhands are cute, but they don't bathe as much as they should and they're wild for our tastes." She smirked. "We like the big, strong, quiet type."

Skye grinned and said, "Prove it."

4

Prove it Mercia did.

Skye enfolded her in his arms as she melted against him, her pliant form one with his, her full breasts mashing into his chest as her pubic mound ground into his organ. She pressed her exquisitely soft lips to his mouth. Her tongue danced with his as her hands ran up and down his sides. His manhood became a pole, straining at his leggings for release, and he felt the familiar flush of rampant lust heat his face.

He placed his hands on her buttocks and pushed her bottom into his loins, relishing the pounding tempo of the racing blood in his veins. Then he let his lips rove over her soft cheeks, chin, and neck, marveling at her exceptionally smooth skin. She moaned lightly and ran her fingers through his hair, knocking off his hat. He didn't mind. His tongue lathered her throat and her warm breath fluttered in his left ear.

"It's been so long," Mercia whispered.

Fargo suddenly scooped her into his arms and hurried down the hall to the bedroom he would occupy. He gently set her down on her back. She surprised him by running her hands over his organ before unbuckling his gunbelt and letting it drop to the floor. Smiling languidly, she busied herself undoing his pants and greedily clutched his engorged iron member in her right hand.

"I can't wait," she said huskily.

"I can," Fargo responded, stretching out beside her. He wanted to savor every moment, not rush things. His tongue dallied at her ear while he unbuttoned the top of her dress and parted the fabric to slip his hand inside. Her undergarments posed little obstruction, and in moments his palm covered her hard little nipple and she panted and squirmed. He worked the nipple between his fingers, feeling her breast swell further, then transferred his hand to her other breast and gave it the same tender treatment. By then Mercia was trying to devour him with fiery nibbles while she writhed in the throes of carnal joy.

His mouth replaced his fingers. He sucked on each nipple, tweaked them with his tongue, and squeezed both mounds until they threatened to burst. She became inflamed, squirming and stroking his pole from top to bottom. Her eyes were closed, her breathing like that of someone who had just run a mile. He lowered his left hand and snaked it under her hiked hem, deliberately refraining from touching her skin until his hand was within inches of her slit. Then, in a quick move that took her unawares and caused her to stiffen and cry out, he clamped his hand between her legs.

"I'm ready, lover," Mercia said. "Ohhhh! I'm ready."

Skye wasn't. He slid his forefinger under her sheer underwear and felt her moist crack part to admit him. She quivered in ecstasy. The slick sides of her womanhood enveloped his finger and for a while he held it motionless while he massaged her globes with his mouth. Her hips began to move, gently at first but with increasing vigor, her mound grinding against his palm. He toyed with her a while longer, then stroked her with his finger. She bucked at the initial plunge and squeezed her legs together.

"Ahhhh! What you do to me!"

Skye was just getting warmed up. He worked his finger in and out for several minutes. Her hands were everywhere under his shirt, alternately rubbing and scratching. When he finally pulled his finger out of her hot hole, she frowned. But the frown changed to a wicked grin as he lowered himself between her legs and removed her underthings. He kissed and licked her thighs and her tummy, then positioned his head at the entrance to her love nest and nuzzled her like a stallion nuzzling a mare. Her legs widened and he poked his stiff tongue into her core.

"I never—!" Mercia exclaimed, and squealed at the top of her lungs.

Fargo licked and probed. Her hands grasped his hair and tried to shove his face halfway up into her womanhood. His cheeks and chin became damp with her tangy juices. His tongue located the tiny knob at the top of her slit and he flicked it mercilessly, driving her to the heights of erotic fulfillment. She moaned loudly now, tossing her head from side to side, and nearly tore his hair out by the roots.

"Suck me, Fargo! I love it!"

He accommodated her, sucking until his mouth and jaw were sore and the bed under her bottom was soaked. Her skin rippled at his merest touch. Her legs swayed, alternately closing on his head and releasing it. When the ache in his jaw became intolerable, he rose to his knees and touched the tip of his pole to her slit. In it went, as easily as a hot knife into butter, and she stiffened and whined.

Skye was about to begin a humping motion when he thought he glimpsed movement in the hall. He glanced around but saw no one. Had Marcia returned early? he wondered, and shrugged. He didn't care if anyone saw them or not. As aroused as he was, he wouldn't stop for anything short of the end of the world.

He pulled his organ partway out, then rammed into her. She screeched, looped her legs around his waist, and clung to him as he pounded furiously away. Sweat caked both of them. The only sound was the slapping of their bodies and the creaking of the bedsprings, a creaking that rose to a grating crescendo as they both neared the summit.

Fargo felt her spend, felt the telltale contractions around his manhood and saw her mouth open seductively and her eyelids flutter. He spurted himself, sinking in her to the hilt and clutching her rear end so he could pump into her depths. The bed bounced so high the legs nearly came off the floor. He threw back his head and shook with the intensity of his release.

"Oh, yessssssssss!" Mercia wailed.

Afterward, he lay by her side and gently ran a finger around each breast. She shivered and cuddled closer.

"I can't believe a man like you hasn't been married yet."

"Don't be getting any notions into that pretty head of yours," Skye advised. "I'm not the marrying kind."

"Pity. You'll make some woman deliriously happy one day."

They lay in each other's arms for several minutes. It was Fargo who roused himself and sat up first. "I'd better get my britches on before your sister comes back."

Mercia giggled. "She might not mind seeing you in the raw. She can be almost as naughty as I am."

"Almost?" Fargo asked as he started making himself presentable.

"I've always been the wild one," Mercia said. "When we were kids I was the one who usually went out behind the woodshed with the boys. Marcia was always too damn shy for her own good."

"Has she ever been with a man?"

"To tell you the truth, I don't rightly know. She doesn't like to talk about her escapades, but I suspect she has once or twice. There was this accountant she cared for a few years back and I know they snuck off every now and then. Where they went, they never said. But Marcia always came back wearing a grin."

"What happened to him?" Fargo absently inquired while strapping on his gunbelt.

"He left her for another girl. It almost broke her heart. She just doesn't take things in stride like I do."

Fargo patted her thigh. "I reckon even identical twins can be as different as night and day inside."

Mercia sat up. "Want me to tell you a secret?"

"About what?"

"How you can tell my sister and me apart."

He looked at her. "You mean there is a way after all?"

"Yep," she said, and began adjusting her underclothes. "Only our parents and Marcia and I knew. When Marcia and I were kids we promised each other never to tell anyone outside the family."

"Won't she be upset if you tell me?"

Mercia shrugged. "We're grown women now. And since you'll be helping us out the next few days, it's only right that you know." She leaned forward and spoke softly. "Besides, I won't inform her that I spilled the beans if you don't."

Fargo sat on the edge of the bed, waiting. He had

studied them both so closely he couldn't imagine any difference he might have missed.

Chuckling, Mercia reached up and tapped her left earlobe. "Take a look at my ears. Notice anything unusual?"

"No. They're both the same."

"But Marcia's aren't. Her left earlobe is smaller than her right one. It's hard to see when she wears her hair long, but when she has it up in a bun you can spot the difference right away. Just don't let on you know our secret."

"I won't," Skye pledged. He heard the front door slam and Marcia call out.

"Mercia? Where are you?"

"Uh-oh," Mercia exclaimed, rising and hastily setting her dress in order. "She might get mad if she finds out I've slept with you. I'll go tell her you're here and that you're resting. Wait a while before you come out."

He watched her hasten away and leaned on his elbow, glad he had agreed to take the job. It was paying off handsomely in unexpected dividends. And if he was lucky Mercia might want a second helping some time soon. He spread out on his back and closed his eyes, intending to rest for a few minutes. But when he next opened them the room was totally dark and he had the feeling that he had slept for an hour or more. From the front office arose the clank of the handpress.

Rising, he walked to the end of the hall. One of the twins was at the press, the other at the desk sorting through papers. Both had their hair pinned up and he could see their earlobes. Sure enough, the woman at the desk had a smaller lobe on the left side. Now he no longer had to guess as to their identities. He stepped into the room.

Mercia spotted him immediately. "Hello, Skye. Did you have a nice nap?"

"I slept too long," Fargo said, and then feigned ignorance so Marcia wouldn't suspect the truth. "Which one are you, anyway?"

"Mercia."

"Are you hungry?" Marcia asked.

"I could eat a horse."

41

"Then I'll fix supper," Marcia volunteered, rising. She headed for a doorway in the west wall.

"Why don't we eat at Ruth's again?" Mercia proposed. "I can use the fresh air and her cooking is better than ours."

Marcia paused and looked at Skye. "I don't mind, but we should leave the decision up to our guest."

"Ruth's it is," Fargo said, and stood by the front door while the women tidied themselves and donned their wraps. He held the door for them, then sauntered out into the refreshing cool air.

Beartown was alive with music, laughter, and loud voices. The saloons were doing brisk business, as they often did once the sun sank. There were dusty horses at most of the hitch rails and people strolling about in the shadows obscuring the boardwalks.

Customers packed the restaurant. Ruth and a waitress were busy taking and filling orders. The hubbub of conversation, audible through the door, swiftly died the instant the twins and Skye entered. All heads snapped up and everyone stared at them.

Fargo moved to a far corner where there were several vacant chairs. Every single customer he passed looked away as if afraid to meet his gaze. He scowled in disgust. They reminded him of sheep in a pen when a wolf comes among them, each afraid that it would be the one the wolf picked to attack. As with most folks who were town born and town bred, they were timid almost to the point of being justifiably branded cowards. Not that they wouldn't defend themselves when set upon. But they were so accustomed to avoiding conflict at all costs, to always doing what was legal and morally right, to being told how to behave by their minister or the local law, that they had nearly lost the capacity to think for themselves in a crisis.

He seated the twins and slid into a chair next to the wall. A tempting idea occurred to him. If he was to shoot into the ceiling, he bet every last person there would flee out the front door in a panic. The good citizens, though, might blame the sisters for his behavior so he folded his arms on the table and satisfied himself with glaring at anyone bold enough to glance toward him.

"Are you in a foul mood?" Marcia inquired.

"Just having some fun," Fargo said.

Mercia laughed. "You have a mean streak in you. I like that in a man."

"You would," Marcia said.

Fargo detected an undercurrent of tension between the pair and reflected on whether he was the cause. Had he inadvertently done something to offend Marcia? They had enough on their minds with the disappearance of their father. He didn't want to add to their problems.

Fortunately, Ruth bustled over, all smiles. "Howdy. I didn't expect to see any of you again until tomorrow."

"We're here for supper," Mercia announced.

"Try the roast and potatoes. They're right tasty if I do say so myself," Ruth said, and bent over the table to speak quietly. "Congratulations. You three are the sole topic of discussion in Beartown." She nodded at Skye. "Especially you, handsome. There are all kinds of rumors flying around. Some people think you've been hired to kill Rory Cord. Others say Lucas and you are both in love with one of the twins and there will be a shootout before long." She snickered. "I haven't seen folks this riled up since the day Bullock tossed young Jess Sinclair into jail for peeping into Mattie Schmidt's window late at night."

"Busybodies," Marcia spat. "They're nothing but busybodies."

"Something eating you, dearie?" Ruth asked.

"Nothing a change in scenery wouldn't cure," Marcia said. "I'm so sick of this town I could scream."

Fargo leaned back. "Why don't you make it roast all around?" he told Ruth. "And this time the meals are on me."

Marcia shot him a blistering look. "How generous. Ruth, you might want to give Skye an extra helping. The poor man must be starved after all he's been through today."

Ruth's brow furrowed but she made no comment. Nodding, she hastened to the kitchen.

Now what the hell was that all about? Fargo wondered. Marcia was definitely angry at him, but for the life of him he couldn't figure out why.

"Marcia, what has gotten into you?" Mercia asked.

"You've been acting rude ever since you came back from collecting. Did one of them give you a hard time?"

"Not at all," Marcia said. "I just have a headache."

They sat in awkward silence while all around them the patrons ate and whispered. Ruth brought their food and glasses of milk.

Fargo picked up his fork and lifted it to jab a succulent piece of meat. He froze on hearing the thunder of many hoofs, as did practically everyone else in the restaurant, until the horses rode on by. He saw the riders out the front window but there wasn't enough light to distinguish details.

"Maybe we shouldn't have come here," Mercia said. "I forgot about Rory Cord."

"He might not even show up," Fargo said, and forked the morsel into his mouth.

"You don't believe that and neither do I," Mercia replied. "He's not the kind of man to forgive and forget. He thinks he has the right to walk all over other people so he does whatever he damn well feels like doing. Our father—." She broke off when a commotion erupted farther down the street.

Fargo placed the fork next to his plate and pushed his chair back from the table. The commotion rapidly grew louder. There were angry shouts and much yelling, just the sort of uproar a sizable mob would make. And they were coming toward the restaurant.

A few customers near the door suddenly stood, deposited money on their table, and dashed into the night. Their action sparked a mass exodus as everyone rose and departed except two gray-haired men and a woman with a young child. The men continued eating as if nothing out of the ordinary had transpired while the woman gazed around the room in confusion, apparently unaware of the reason for the flight.

Boots rapped on the boardwalk just outside and a cluster of men approached the entrance. The door had been left wide open by one of the fleeing customers, and into the doorway stalked a huge man in a brown hat, a white shirt, and black pants.

Fargo didn't need to be told that this was Rory Cord. One look at the man's cruel features, which resembled those of a mean-spirited bulldog, was enough to enable him to put two and two together and match the brutish figure with everything he had heard about Cord's disposition. He casually lowered his right hand to his thigh within inches of the Colt.

Cord swept the restaurant with his close-set brown eyes as he advanced a couple of yards, then halted. The stub of a cigar was crammed in the corner of his mouth and he now took it out and glared at Skye. Cowhands filed in behind him and fanned out. Foremost among them was Tillman, his jaw swollen and discolored.

"You must be Fargo," Cord declared, growling his words.

"What of it?" Skye responded.

"You're the bastard who beat up my son and did a number on Tillman here," Cord said in contempt. "And you're the one who shot young Clem for having a little fun."

"Dragging a man by a rope isn't my idea of fun."

"It doesn't matter what you think," Cord said, taking a few strides. "In case you ain't heard, I'm Rory Cord and I pretty much run this territory. I own the biggest ranch west of Fort Laramie. Ask anyone and they'll tell you that crossing me is a dumb thing to do."

"I've heard you're the cock of the roost," Fargo said.

Cord grinned and puffed out his chest. "Then you'll understand I can't let you get away with what you did to my boy and my men. If I let you ride off, every saddle tramp who comes down the trail will think they can walk all over my outfit and nothing will happen. You see that, don't you?"

"Your boy was in the wrong."

"Doesn't matter. If anyone is going to thrash Lucas it will be me."

Mercia stood, her fists clenched. "Your boy, as you so quaintly call that animal, was manhandling me. Skye Fargo did the right thing by intervening."

Cord didn't even look at her. "This is between Fargo and me, woman. Butt the hell out."

"Is that any way to talk to a lady?" Mercia snapped. "No wonder your son is an animal. He takes after you."

A red tinge crept into Cord's cheeks and he shifted his glare to her. "And you're just like your father. You talk big but you hide behind your skirts just like your pa hid behind that printing press of his. You figure you can insult folks and they won't slap you around because you're a woman." He jammed the cigar back into his mouth and spoke through partly clenched teeth. "Your pa figured he could insult folks and then claim he had the right to do it because he was a rotton journalist."

Mercia trembled with rage. "If I were a man I'd shove those words back down your throat."

"But you ain't, woman," Cord said, leering. "So why don't you close that mouth of yours and let me finish my business with Fargo."

"Leave him alone. I'm warning you," Mercia said.

Cord laughed and most of his men joined in the mirth. "Now I'm scared! We'll turn around and ride back to the ranch right this minute." He looked at Skye. "On your feet. You're coming with us."

"Like hell I am," Fargo answered, easing his right hand nearer to his .44.

"What are you worried about?" Cord asked, and chuckled. "I don't mean you no harm. Why, all I came here for was to give you an invite."

"An invitation?" Fargo asked skeptically.

"Yep," Cord answered, then barked, "Charley!"

A pudgy cowhand moved from behind Cord's back. In his right hand was a coiled lariat.

Cord's humor evaporated and he glowered wickedly at Skye. "I came to invite you to a necktie party."

5

A total and tension-laced hush fell over the restaurant.

It was the woman with the child who broke the deathly stillness. She scooped her offspring into her arms, dropped coins down for their meals, and went out with her head lowered and her arms clasped protectively around her daughter. The cowhands moved aside for her, then resumed their original positions, forming a wall between Fargo and the doorway.

Skye noticed that Ruth had materialized out of the kitchen and was off to one side, her apron clutched in her hands. She was safely out of the line of fire, but not so the twins. "Mercia," he said softly, "why don't Marcia and you move over by the far wall. I don't want either of you catching a slug."

"We're not budging," Mercia said. "If this vermin wants you he'll have to go through us."

Cord paid no attention to her. He seemed perplexed as he said to Skye, "You're not thinking of resisting? Can't you see you're outnumbered ten to one? These boys will cut you down before you get off two shots."

"Maybe," Fargo said, standing slowly, his right hand almost touching the Colt. "But I reckon I can fire three or four times before they nail me, and every single bullet has your name on it."

The idea didn't appeal to Cord. He chewed on his cigar and stared at Skye's Colt. "The word is that you're quite good with that six-shooter."

"Come any closer and you'll find out just how good."

"But I'm unarmed," Cord noted, indicating there was no gunbelt strapped around his waist.

"A man shouldn't go around making threats he's not prepared to back up," Fargo said, and thought of a way

47

to create a rift between Cord and the cowhands. "Or did you figure your men would do all the dying for you?"

Some of the cowhands cast questioning gazes at their employer.

"I've always heard that a man should never ask others to do something he wouldn't do himself," Fargo said, adding icing to the cake. "That is, if he's a *real* man and not a coward at heart."

More of the cowhands were looking at Rory.

"I'm no coward!" Cord barked.

Fargo smiled. He had Cord right where he wanted him. "Prove it," he said. "You say you have a beef with me, then let's settle it man to man, here and now."

Cord hesitated until he glanced at his men. He read the situation instantly and knew if he refused the challenge he would lose his claim to undisputed leadership. With a shrug he reverted to his typical arrogant self and responded, "It makes no nevermind to me how I pay you back. If you want me to pound you to a pulp, be my guest."

"And your men won't interfere, no matter what happens?" Fargo asked.

"You have my word on it."

From the entrance came another voice. "And I'll make sure that they don't."

As one, the cowhands and Cord pivoted. Marshal Fred Bullock stood with his boots firmly planted and a double-barreled shotgun in his hands. He hefted the weapon, then cocked both hammers. The men nearest to the doorway, keenly aware of the destructive power of buckshot at close range, backed away.

"Rory," Bullock said, "didn't Burt tell you I don't want any more trouble in Beartown?"

"He told me," Cord said sullenly.

"Yet you rode in anyway," Bullock said, glancing at the rope. "And you have the gall to set yourself up as judge, jury, and executioner of an innocent man." He pointed the shotgun at Cord. "I won't tolerate vigilante justice in my jurisdiction, not even from you."

"I'll remember how you've treated me when your term of office is up."

Bullock wasn't intimidated. "If you're going to fight Fargo, get on with it."

Skye walked around the table. He didn't want to fight indoors where he wouldn't have as much room to maneuver. Nor did he want Ruth's furniture damaged. "How about if we do this outdoors?" he suggested.

"Wherever," Cord said.

Marshal Bullock led the exodus, backing well out into the street so he could cover the cowhands as they emerged. They gathered in a group at the corner of the building. The twins and Ruth moved to the left and stopped next to the window.

Fargo trailed Rory Cord outside. He unbuckled his gunbelt and handed it to Mercia, then stepped off the boardwalk to confront his enemy. Cord would be difficult to beat. The man was as solid as a redwood and possessed wide shoulders and rippling neck muscles. Cord's hands were more like grizzly paws, the knuckles like knots on a tree.

"Lucas was feeling too poorly to bring along tonight," Cord said. "Too bad. He would have liked to see you begging for mercy."

"Never happen," Fargo said, and made the mistake of looking at a lantern in a window across the way that cast a feeble glow on both of them. The world exploded as Rory delivered a lightning right uppercut that caught him on the chin and lifted him clear off his feet. He crashed onto his back, dimly hearing cheers from the cowhands and the thud of Cord's boots as the rancher rushed him. Twisting, he got both hands flat on the ground and went to rise when a boot slammed into his ribs and sent him rolling.

"That's the way, boss!" someone shouted. "Bust every bone in his body!"

Skye lunged upright, a searing pang racking his side. He wondered if a rib or two might indeed be broken and raised his arms to protect himself from another assault. Cord came on like an enraged bull, his head held low, his neck bunched to absorb punches, his malletlike fists poised to strike. Skye adroitly sidestepped a blow aimed at his face and countered with a punch to the stomach, but it was like hitting a thick board. The man's stomach was a mass of muscle.

Rory Cord's lips curled. "If that's the best you can do, mister, this won't last long." He swung a looping left.

Blocking, Fargo tried to connect with a right but was readily countered. He retreated bit by bit as Cord rained a flurry of calculated blows, and although he warded them off, his forearms ached from absorbing the driving fury behind each punch.

Word of the fight was spreading all up and down Beartown with men going from saloon to saloon to spread the news or yelling up to curious citizens who had poked their heads out of windows to find out what all the ruckus was about. People hurried toward the restaurant to see for themselves, many bringing their children along to watch.

Fargo was vaguely aware of all the activity. He barely deflected a punch to the side of his head and glided to the right. Whipping his shoulder forward to add force to his swing, he rammed his fist into Cord's side. The man never so much as grunted.

On the boardwalk the twins were offering encouragement, Mercia bouncing up and down in her excitement.

He ducked under a wild hook and too late saw Cord's knee sweeping at his face. Only by suddenly turning his head sideways was he able to avoid the brunt of the blow. Still, the knee glanced off his cheek, dazing him, and he swayed.

Cord, thinking he was seconds away from victory, confidently closed in.

"Look out!" one of the twins screamed.

Fargo didn't need the warning. He slipped a right on the outside, jabbed twice into Cord's ribs, then shifted and connected with a straight punch to Cord's mouth. Like a butterfly, Skye flitted backward out of reach of the rancher's shorter arms and set himself. If he couldn't match Cord for sheer strength, he would rely upon speed and agility and the razor instincts he had honed in the wild.

Blood trickled from Cord's split lower lip. He paused to wipe the back of his hand across his mouth. "You were lucky, scum. It won't happen again."

Only it did. Fargo saw to that by sliding to the left when Cord went for his torso and jabbing twice more in swift succession. Again he hit Cord's mouth. More blood gushed forth. The rancher, livid, lunged and flailed with his right and left.

Skye dropped into a crouch, the blows sailed overhead, and he shot up like a ball out of a cannon, both arms straight, his elbows locked. His knuckles smacked into the underside of Cord's chin and the huge man tottered. Once more Skye used jabs to his advantage, delivering four to Cord's middle before the rancher moved away.

"Damn your hide," Cord snarled.

The crowd, Fargo realized, had fallen silent. Even the cowhands were watching quietly. Perhaps this was the first time they had ever seen anyone hold his own against their employer, he reflected, and the moment's distraction cost him. A hammer seemed to slam into the right side of his head. Stars burst before his eyes. His knees buckled and he started to sag. Halfway down another hammer drove into his gut with the force of a mule kick. The air whooshed from his lungs and he doubled over, his forehead striking the hard ground at the same moment as his knees. He tried to control the pain and sucked air deep into his lungs. Helpless, he tensed for the beating he was sure to receive. Oddly, for a few seconds nothing happened. Then the toe of a boot nudged his side.

"I want you to suffer, Fargo. I want you to know the end is coming and not be able to do a thing about it."

Skye was gripped under the shoulders and hauled erect. Cord's arms looped around his and he felt Cord's knuckles dig into his spine as Cord clasped those huge hands. He was face to face with the rancher, held effortlessly as if he was a child instead of a grown man.

"I've killed with my hands before," Cord disclosed. "Broke their backs just like I'm going to break yours." He smiled, then abruptly tightened his hold, his arms like twin boa constrictors.

Fargo stiffened as excruciating agony streaked up and down his spinal column. He could well believe Cord's boast. The man was unbelievably strong. He was being slowly but inexorably crushed to death and unless he broke free quickly he would soon suffer a snapped backbone.

"Where's all your bluster now?" Cord rasped, the veins on his neck bulging as he applied more and more pressure.

Dizziness assailed Skye. He bowed his head, closed his eyes, and tapped his reservoir of strength for enough to extricate himself. But when he thrust his arms outward they barely moved. Cord chortled, his face beet red from his exertion. In desperation Skye tried again with the same result. His spine was in torment, on the verge of being shattered. He must do something and do it immediately.

Somewhere along the line he had lost his hat again. Just as well. It would only have gotten in the way when he made his move, which he now did by whipping his head up and around. He winced at the contact of his head with Cord's chin. Teeth crunched and blood splattered onto his brow. Viciously he swung his head from side to side, pounding Cord's square chin twice more with his temples. Cord's grip loosened but not yet enough, so he drew his head back and arced his temple onto the rancher's nose. There was a loud snap. Cord roared, let go, and shoved, and Skye nearly tripped over his own feet as he stumbled backward.

Rory Cord pressed a hand to his broken nose. "You son of a bitch!" he shouted.

Fargo was far from through. He glided in and lashed out with a right, a left, and a right, scoring with all three. Cord belatedly rallied and swung, but Fargo blocked the punch and socked the man twice on the mouth. For a second Cord carelessly let his arms fall. Skye was ready. He drew his right fist back as far as he could, then swept his fist into Cord's face, putting all of his weight and all the power in his steely sinews into the blow.

Rory Cord rocked on his heels, blinked in blank astonishment, and crashed onto his back in the middle of the street. A tiny cloud of dust rose into the air, then settled onto his battered features and clothes.

Fargo stared down at his foe, half expecting the man to rise again. Finally convinced he had won, he turned and shuffled toward the restaurant. His head hurt. His body hurt. His ribs throbbed worst of all. He spied his hat lying in his path and leaned down to pick it up. The simple motion made him stagger like a drunk, but he got the hat on his head, then stopped short on realizing he was walking toward Cord's cowhands instead of the twins.

"This settles it," Marshal Bullock announced, appearing on Skye's right. "I want you boys to take your boss back to the RC. When he comes around you let him know that if he rides back into Beartown any time soon he'd better not come in looking to stir things up again. Understood?"

"Yep," Tillman answered. "We'll tell him but I'm not making any promises." He glanced at Skye. "The boss won't take this lying down."

"He'd be smart to let it drop," Bullock said, and wagged his shotgun at the unconscious Cord. "Now get going."

Fargo watched the ranch hands lift Cord and carry him down the street to a hitching rail.

The marshal looked at him and grinned. "I thought for sure you were a goner when he got his arms around you. You're one tough hombre."

"Right now I feel like mush," Fargo said. He stepped onto the boardwalk and leaned on a post. The townspeople began to drift off, murmuring among themselves, many gazing at him in undisguised amazement.

"Here's your gunbelt," Mercia said.

Skye took it. His fingers felt stiff and slightly swollen as he buckled the belt around his waist. He hoped his right hand wouldn't swell too badly. Although he had beaten Rory Cord, and despite Bullock's warnings, there would be more trouble. And if he couldn't draw and shoot he'd be easy prey for anyone wanting to finish him off.

Marcia moved in front of him, aglow with excitement. "You were marvelous!" she declared. "You gave him exactly what he deserved! Maybe now the Cords and their men will leave us alone."

"I wouldn't count on it," Mercia said.

A rumble in Fargo's stomach reminded him that his meal had been rudely interrupted. "I'm starved," he said, and went in. The restaurant was deserted, but that soon changed when the twins, Ruth, and the marshal filed inside. The roast was still warm. He filled his mouth and chewed gingerly, his jaw lanced by mild pangs.

"You have blood all over your face," Ruth commented. "Want me to fetch a washbasin and a cloth for you?"

"I'll wash up later," Fargo responded with his mouth full. "But thanks."

Bullock had halted near the doorway. "I reckon I'll be off. If there's anything I can do for you, let me know." He tipped his hat to the ladies and was gone.

"Perhaps I've misjudged him," Mercia said thoughtfully.

"Me, too," Marcia added. "Maybe he's on our side after all."

Ruth shook her head. "Fred is on the side of the law. Some folks laugh at him behind his back, but when all is said and done he's as impartial a lawman as you're likely to find anywhere and he does his job well."

Fargo listened to their ensuing discussion about the state of affairs in Beartown with half an ear. He was more interested in filling his stomach and getting a good night's sleep. Tomorrow he intended to search north of town for clues to the disappearance of Adam Whitman.

Drowsiness set in once Skye was done. He swallowed the last of the roast and sat back, wishing he had a stiff drink instead of a glass of milk. But Ruth didn't sell liquor, so he downed the glass in great gulps, then slowly stood. "What time do you open in the morning?"

"Six A.M.," Ruth answered. "It used to be five but I've gotten lazy in my old age."

"I'll be here for some bacon and eggs," Fargo said, and reached into his pocket for money to pay for the meals. The twins had spent so much time talking that their plates were only half empty.

Mercia glanced up at him. "You shouldn't go anywhere in the shape you're in. Wait another day. Give yourself time to rest and heal."

"I start hunting tomorrow," Fargo insisted. "Right now I want to hit the sack. Your front door is unlocked, isn't it?"

"Yes," Marcia said.

"Then I'll see you ladies in the morning," Fargo said. He walked out into the cool night, inhaled deeply, and listened. Beartown was unusually quiet. No music or loud laughter came from the saloons. There were few people abroad and few horses at the hitching rails. The RC outfit had ridden out shortly after the fight and without the cowhands to liven things up the town was a shadow of its normal self.

He draped his right hand over his Colt and crossed the street to the Whitman residence. The pain in his ribs had subsided enough so he could manage without difficulty. Six feet from the front door he halted, drew the .44, and crouched.

The door was ajar.

Skye specifically recalled opening it for the twins when they went to eat and remembered closing it behind them. Either someone had stopped by, found the sisters gone, and left, or else there was someone inside at that very moment, perhaps waiting to bushwhack them. He preferred to err on the side of caution. Moving to the left, he approached the corner, the Colt leveled. The lanterns in the newspaper office were glowing brightly and he could see the office clearly. No one was in there.

He worked his way to the rear of the house. No sounds issued from within, nor did he see anyone through the windows he passed. The back door was closed. He tried the latch, then lifted it as slowly and softly as possible. The top hinge creaked lightly when he gently eased the door inward with his foot. He could see along the hallway to the office, and the hall was empty.

Exercising stealth, he moved forward, planning to double-check the office and then head upstairs. He came abreast of his room when the door was suddenly yanked open and a vague figure loomed in the dark.

6

In a twinkling Skye Fargo whirled. His thumb pulled back the hammer with a distinct click, yet even as it did the figure threw his arms overhead and cried out in fright.

"Don't shoot, Fargo! Don't shoot! It's me, Grundel."

Skye let his trigger finger relax but held the revolver steady. "You damn fool," he snapped. "Are you tired of living?"

"No, sir," the bearded cowhand said, dropping his arms. "I had to talk to you and didn't want anyone to see me so I snuck on in here a while ago." He paused. "Word down at the saloon was that you were staying with the twins."

"Why aren't you with the rest of your outfit?"

Grundel moved into the hallway. "I'm getting quit of them. I don't like the way things are shaping up around here and I'm not anxious to die for the Cords. I hired on to work cattle, not tangle with the likes of you. You're not like that newspaper fella."

"What do you know about Whitman?" Fargo asked, lowering his gun.

"The fool should have left well enough alone. But he didn't cotton to Rory and nosed around where he had no business being. I wasn't there when they caught him but I heard stories."

"What happened? Tell me everything."

"I've already told you more than I can without getting myself killed. But I will tell you this," Grundel said, and spoke so softly the words were almost inaudible. "If you want to find out what happened to him, nose around the RC."

"Why? Did Rory Cord kill him?"

"You'll have to learn the truth for yourself," Grundel said.

Fargo was annoyed. "Why did you bother to sneak in here if you're not going to help me?"

"I don't care one way or the other about the newspaperman. But I do care about my skin, and I don't want you thinking I had any part in the plan Tillman came up with to do you away." Grundel glanced at the front and back doors. "Tillman was mad as a wet hen after you beat Rory. As the boys were getting set to ride off, I heard Tillman tell them he's expecting you to show up at the ranch before too long. He plans to post lookouts who will report to him when you do. Then they'll hunt you down and get revenge for Lucas and Rory."

"I can take care of myself."

Grundel nodded. "Better than most, too. Which is why I'm lighting out of this neck of the country as soon as I collect my back wages from Tillman."

"Why don't you tell what you know to the marshal?" Fargo proposed. If he could persuade Grundel to talk it would save him a lot of time and effort.

"Bullock ain't no match for the Cords. They might make him tell where he heard about Whitman's interest in the RC before they killed him, then they'd stake me out and peel off my hide with a Bowie knife. No, sir. I aim to live for quite a few years yet."

Fargo debated whether to try and force more information out of the cowhand. Clearly Grundel knew more. A few whacks with the Colt might loosen his lips. But Grundel had risked his life by coming to the house to warn him and it wouldn't be fair to repay the man by beating him.

"I'll be on my way," Grundel said, stepping to the back door. He stopped and glanced over his shoulder. "Maybe I do owe you a little more. You could have killed me when I tried to draw on you and you didn't."

Fargo waited.

"Don't trust nobody. Not a soul. Things ain't as they seem. There's more to the feud than most know."

"What do—?" Fargo began, and fell silent when Grundel darted out. He walked to the doorway but the cowhand was gone. What had he meant by a feud? And who had been feuding? Whitman and Rory Cord? He closed the door and went to his room, sank wearily onto the bed, and attempted to fit the pieces of the puzzle together. The task was hopeless. Grundel had told him a lot, and yet very little. Only one conclusion was obvious. Whitman's disappearance involved much more than a minor squabble over a few critical editorials. And by agreeing to help the sisters he was stirring up a hornet's nest of trouble. Now all he had to do was keep from being stung.

Dawn tinged the eastern sky with vivid pink and crimson hues when Fargo rode out of Beartown, heading north. A brisk wind fanned his face and prompted him to pull his hat down tighter to keep it from being blown off. The passage of countless horses and wagons had worn a dirt track that wended in the general direction of the RC spread and he followed it for the first three miles. All around was flat land covered with sagebrush and grass. Once, off in the distance, a herd of pronghorn antelope interrupted their grazing to warily watch him go by. Several times he spooked rabbits that bounded off in frantic, prodigious leaps.

This was the land he loved, the untamed land where animals and man could roam free and live as they pleased. Whether towering mountains, virgin forest, or limitless prairie, he called it all home. He would rather spend a day in the wild than a year in any town or city. They were simply too confining. He felt uncomfortable in them after a while, eager for the open spaces that stretched for as far as the eye could see.

So he smiled in satisfaction as he rode on, his lake blue eyes probing potential spots where a concealed rifleman might try to pick him off. He took Grundel's warning seriously, and even though Grundel had said the RC outfit planned to bushwhack him on or near the ranch, he wasn't taking anything for granted. They might try sooner.

Low hills appeared and the road wound among them. Rather than stick to the road, where he would be an easy target for someone posted higher up, he angled to the west and took a game trail to the crest of the first hill. A panoramic view of the countryside unfolded. He discovered the hills extended for over a mile. Beyond lay a wide, green valley, and it was there, he figured that the RC ranch was situated.

For the next hour he rode slowly northward, sticking to the high ground as much as possible, noting landmarks and the locations of the few streams that watered the region. Now and then he would glimpse the Bear River to the west.

There was only one hill left to cross and he was starting down the slope directly opposite it when he spotted a flash of light at the top in the midst of a cluster of boulders. Instantly he reined to the left and used every available cover until he was at the bottom. Then, swinging west, he skirted the last hill until he was on the far side from the road.

Dismounting, he took the reins in his left hand and hiked upward. When he was less than fifty yards from the crest, he tied the Ovaro to a stunted tree, drew the Colt, and stealthily crept higher. Like the Indians among whom he had lived, he climbed silently, avoiding all twigs and loose rocks that might give his presence away.

A shift in the breeze brought him the acrid scent of cigarette smoke. He halted behind a bush and studied the boulders above until he saw a puff of smoke drifting skyward from a spot near the east side of the cluster. Then, keeping low, he came up on the boulders from the west, placing each foot lightly down before applying his full weight.

He reached the boulders and heard someone cough. Easing to the north, he worked his way around until an opening presented itself between two boulders as large as his horse. Stepping into the opening, he extended the Colt and moved on cat feet into the heart of the cluster. Someone sighed and muttered inaudible words. The scent of the cigarette smoke became stronger, so strong he resisted an impulse to cough. And then, inching around a square block bigger than himself, he gazed down the back of a cowhand seated on a stone bench. The man was watching the dirt road below, and propped against the bench was a rifle.

"Howdy," Fargo said, cocking the Colt.

Startled, the man stiffened and went to grab the rifle.

"I wouldn't do that if I was you," Fargo advised. "This Colt of mine has a hair trigger."

59

The man imitated the stone on which he sat, his right arm outstretched. "Who are you? What do you want?"

"You know who I am," Fargo said.

"Don't do anything you'll regret," the cowhand said.

Fargo moved to the right until he could see the man's swarthy face. "I don't much like it when folks set out to try and kill me," he commented, and glowered. "It makes me mad."

"I don't know what you're talking about. I'm hunting deer, is all."

Without warning Fargo took a step and swiped the barrel of the Colt across the cowhand's face, knocking the man to the ground. As the bushwhacker tried to rise, Fargo moved in again and hit him on the temple. The man's legs buckled and he sprawled on his stomach, stunned.

"I can't abide liars, either," he said, and leaned down to take the cowhand's revolver and fling it far down the slope. The rifle got the same treatment. Then he made himself comfortable on the bench and surveyed the valley.

Rory Cord had selected the site for his ranch wisely. Grass in abundance promised feed for hundreds if not thousands of cattle. There were two narrow creeks for water. And a dozen or better stands of timber provided ample lumber.

Fargo could see over a hundred mingled cows and bulls from his vantage point. He remembered Ruth telling him that Cord had brought in five hundred head from Texas about two years ago, so he guessed there must be six or seven hundred by now. Not being a cowman, Fargo knew only what he had learned during his extensive travels, which was more than most men. The cattle he could see were all longhorns, the variety found exclusively in Texas, confirming Ruth's account. Since they were grouped in the open range and not back in the brush, he concluded these were second or third generation range-broke cattle rather than true wild longhorns. The wild ones stuck to the heavy brush and were as fierce as grizzlies. A man who roped one put his life on the line.

At the center of the valley stood the ranch house, a long bunkhouse, and the barn, ringed on three sides by trees. Vague figures were moving about near a wooden fence flanking the barn.

The bushwhacker groaned and slowly sat up. A jagged gash in his left cheek and a cut on his temple were both rimmed with seeping blood. He looked at Skye and scowled. "Damn you, mister, for what you've done to me!"

"You had it coming," Fargo replied. "Count your blessings that you're alive." He stood and stretched. "Now take off your boots."

The cowhand blinked. "What?"

"Are you hard of hearing as well as stupid? I said to take off your boots."

"What the hell for?"

Fargo aimed the Colt at the man's midsection. "Don't tempt me. I'd shoot you right now if I had proof you were involved with Adam Whitman's disappearance. As it is I'm letting you off easy."

The man stared at the business end of the .44 for a moment, then at Skye's face. Muttering under his breath, he began removing his boots. "You're all wrong about this affair, mister. Cord didn't have anything to do with that newspaperman who went missing."

"How do you know?" Fargo asked.

"The boss told us so himself four days ago. He gathered all of us hands in the bunkhouse and explained there was talk going around town tying him to the disappearance. He said we weren't to pay any attention to it, that there had been bad blood between Whitman and him but he hadn't stooped so low as to kill the bastard."

"How long have you worked for Cord?"

"Over a year. He's a hard man, but he's fair. He doesn't shirk work like some bosses I've known, and he'll go out of his way to help any of his hands who need it. We're all loyal to the brand, mister. If you go up against him, you go up against us."

Fargo didn't like the sound of that. He didn't want to tangle with innocent cowhands who saw him as a threat to their employer and their ranch. "When you get back tell your friends that I have nothing against them, but I've promised the Whitman twins I would try and find out what happened to their pa. If no one interferes there won't be any problem."

The man had his boots off. His right sock had a hole in it through which his big toe protruded. He now stared at the toe and wiggled it, then looked up at Skye. "I'll tell them but it won't make a difference. If we catch you snooping on the RC we'll shoot you on sight."

"Is that what you were fixing to do right here?" Fargo asked, standing.

"No, sir," the cowhand replied. "I was told to keep a lookout and when you came along the road to signal the ranch house with my pocket mirror. They'd take it from there."

Fargo believed him. It tied in with Grundel's information. "All right. On your feet and start walking."

The cowhand glanced toward the ranch. "All the way back with no boots on? It'll take an hour or better. I'm not used to going afoot. Anywhere I have to go, I go on horseback."

"Thanks for the reminder," Fargo said, scanning the slope below. "Where did you hide your horse?"

"I don't have it with me," the cowhand blatantly lied, his eyes darting to a stand of trees twenty yards lower to the northeast.

"Sure you don't," Fargo said. "And thanks again." He nodded at the stand. "You can come back and get your horse later. Head on out."

The hand stood. "We'll get you, Trailsman. You'll see."

Fargo motioned toward the road below. "You're wasting time. And try not to step on anything prickly."

Mumbling curses, the man pivoted and began to descend, stepping gingerly, his arms outstretched as if for extra balance. Several times before reaching the bottom he stepped on something that made him hop and curse aloud, and once he reached the road he gazed up at Skye and angrily shook his fist.

Smiling, Fargo gave a wave and watched the irate cowhand head toward the ranch. He waited until the man had gone a quarter of a mile before he holstered the Colt and quickly returned to the Ovaro. If he was right, Rory Cord would head for the hill once the hand arrived at the ranch and reported the incident. And if he was lucky, every last cowhand would be called on to tag along. Which gave him about an hour to get into position.

He rode to the base of the hill and turned to the northwest, making for the creek on the west side of the ranch. For a short span between the hills and the creek he was in the open and he crossed the space swiftly in the hope no one would spot him. Once among the trees and dense brush lining the bank he followed the creek to the north until he came abreast of the ranch house. Along the way he saw scores of cattle, none of which paid him any mind.

He wound up approximately two miles west of the buildings. Scattered stands of trees, like islands in a sea of grass, offered a risky means of getting closer. Shucking the Sharps from its scabbard, he touched his spurs to the stallion's flanks and galloped to the nearest group of evergreens. After a thorough scrutiny he rode to the next, and then the next, and on and on until he arrived at some firs within three hundred yards of the barn.

Swinging down, Fargo secured the reins to a branch and edged to a tree from where he commanded an unobstructed view of the ranch proper. A few hands were at the corral watching another man attempt to break an ornery mare. There was no sign of the Cords. Since it would be awhile before the cowhand from the hill got there, Fargo made himself comfortable on the ground with his shoulder against the trunk.

Half an hour elapsed. A cricket chirped nearby. A fly pestered him until he gave it a swat that flipped it into a patch of weeds. The sharp movement aggravated his battered ribs. They had been aching all day and the pain had flared briefly after he struck the cowhand, but he didn't feel they were broken. Still, he had to remember to take it easy.

A shout at the buildings drew his attention. Shuffling toward the ranch house was the footsore cowhand. Others were rushing toward him from the barn, the corral, and the bunkhouse. The front door to the Cord house opened and out came Rory and Lucas. Everyone gathered around the lookout.

He saw words exchanged and angry gestures. Rory Cord issued orders and every man there ran for his horse. Within three minutes they were all saddled and mounted, and at a wave from Rory they raced off to the south, raising a considerable dust cloud in their wake.

The plan had worked perfectly.

Fargo hurried to the pinto and mounted. He scoured the buildings once more, then galloped toward them. His purpose in luring the Cords and the ranch hands away was so he could check the corral and the barn for the bay and the saddle belonging to Adam Whitman. It was a long shot and he didn't expect to hit pay dirt, but he had to try. Whitman's bay sported a white blaze on its forehead that would make it easy to identify and the saddle was a fancy English version Whitman had bought back East. No cowhand in his right mind would own one since he would be made a laughingstock, so if there was an English saddle on the premises it must belong to the journalist. Mercia had assured Skye she could tell her father's saddle at a glance and he had promised to bring it back with him if he found it.

The ranch appeared deserted as he rode up but he kept his thumb on the rifle hammer on the off chance one of the hands had been left behind. He checked the horses in the corral first. None were bays. Moving to the open barn doors, he slid to the ground and jammed the Sharps in its scabbard to free his hand for using the Colt. At close range the revolver was better; it was lighter, easier to use, and contained more rounds.

A third of the stalls in the barn were empty. He walked down the middle aisle, searching to the right and the left. He halted on finding a bay but was disappointed to see it lacked the distinctive blaze marking. A complete check showed no other bays or any English saddles. His long shot had been a bust.

Fargo retraced his steps to the doors, turned to give the interior of the barn another sweep, and felt his blood run cold when a weapon was cocked directly behind him.

"I have a shotgun, mister. Let that pistol drop or I'll blow you in half."

7

It was a woman's voice.

Even so, Fargo did as he was told. A woman armed with a shotgun was equally as dangerous as a man, perhaps more so since many women were unfamiliar with firearms or rarely used them. He released the Colt and heard it thud onto the ground. Making a point of holding his arms straight out so the woman could see he wasn't going to try anything and wouldn't get trigger happy, he said, "Whatever you want is fine by me."

"I should think it would be, unless you're a bigger fool than most people say."

"Can I turn around?"

"Slowly. I'd hate to get nervous and accidentally squeeze this trigger. There'd be blood and guts all over the place and I'd be the one who has to clean it up."

Was she making fun of him? Skye wondered as he pivoted and regarded his captor. She appeared to be in her mid-to-late-forties, about the same age as Rory Cord. Streaks of gray marked her otherwise black hair, which she had up in a bun. Her plain features reflected a sort of inner dignity that was accented by the steely fire in her brown eyes. "I take it you know who I am?"

"The Trailsman, they call you. Skye Fargo."

"You're one up on me. Who might you be?"

"I'm Rebecca Cord, Rory's wife."

Fargo calmly met her level gaze. She undoubtedly knew he had beaten Rory in a fistfight and might harbor a grudge. He didn't dare do anything to antagonize her. "What do you plan to do with me?"

"I don't rightly know yet. I could hold you here until my husband comes back. He'd like to get his hands on you after what you did to him. No one has ever bested him with fists before. You must be a heck of a scrapper."

"Did he tell you why we fought?"

"He didn't have to. It was because of what you did to Lucas," Rebecca said accusingly. "I don't understand why you picked a fight with Lucas, though."

"No one has told you about the Whitman twins?"

A cloud seemed to envelop Rebecca's features. "What about them?"

"The whole trouble started when I saw Lucas manhandling one of them. I stopped him and he didn't like it, so later he came looking for me in Ruth Heatherton's restaurant," Fargo explained. Her face betrayed no emotion and it was impossible for him to gauge her reaction. He went on. "As for your husband, he rode into Beartown fixing to hang me. If I hadn't talked him into fighting me man to man, right about now I'd be swinging from a tree on the outskirts of town."

"I see," Rebecca said.

"I'm not out to get your family, ma'am," Fargo said. "All I'm interested in is finding out what happened to Adam Whitman and I have cause to believe your husband might know the answer."

"My Rory didn't kill that snoop," Rebecca stated flatly. "The Good Lord knows Rory isn't a saint, but he's never killed an unarmed man and Adam Whitman never carried a gun."

"He didn't?" Fargo responded. This was news to him. He had naturally assumed, as would any man who spent his life on the raw edge of the frontier, that Whitman owned a pistol.

"No, sir. From what I heard, Whitman didn't believe in guns. Said that civilized men had no reason toting one."

That fit, Fargo reflected. Whitman was from the East, and many easterners entertained mistaken notions about life in the West. Since they had been brought up in towns and cities where the wearing of firearms was illegal, they tended to regard those who did wear guns as ruffians or worse. And since they had never found their lives in any danger, they came to think that they could handle any difficulty without having to resort to force.

"You're barking up the wrong tree if you figure Rory murdered Adam Whitman," Rebecca said.

"Maybe so, but the Whitman girls think differently."

"They both said that?"

"They both know your husband and their father weren't on the best of terms."

Then Rebecca Cord did a strange thing. She took a step nearer and jabbed the shotgun at the ground, as if striking someone or something, and hissed, "That hussy! I should have known!"

"Ma'am?" Fargo said, puzzled by her behavior and her statement. Who was a hussy? Mercia or Marcia or both? And why?

Rebecca went to speak when the distant sound of approaching horses made her glance to the south.

Fargo did the same and felt his pulse quicken. Galloping toward the ranch house were the Cords and their hands. By all rights they should have been halfway to the hills by now! What were they doing coming back? Had they spotted him somehow?

"Mister, you'd best grab that six-shooter of yours and skedaddle," Rebecca said, lowering her shotgun. "I don't want your blood on my hands, and if my husband catches you he'll put a rope around your neck and haul you off to the nearest tree."

There were a dozen questions Fargo wanted to ask her, but he didn't have time. He scooped up the Colt and slid it into his holster, then darted to the Ovaro and swung up. Pausing, he stared at her and smiled. "Thank you."

"Thank the Good Lord, not me. Now get!," Rebecca said, and added in a pleading tone, "And leave us be from here on out. Please!"

Skye hauled on the reins and rode due west. He saw the RC outfit slant toward him. Spurring the stallion to go faster, he raced around the closest stand of trees on the far side from his pursuers, and the moment he was out of their sight he changed course, riding due north. If Cord and the others suspected he had gone into the trees and would open fire on them from concealment, the outfit might stop or slow down to make a cautious circuit of the stand. Either way he had gained a few precious minutes.

To the north lay open range, then more hills. If he could reach them he stood a fair chance of eluding Cord and company. There were cattle everywhere and he hoped he wouldn't accidentally spook any of them into stampeding. To his relief, they almost totally ignored him.

Skye repeatedly glanced over his shoulder. Several minutes went by, his lead widening with each passing second. Then there came a shout and he looked back to see riders sweeping around both ends of the stand. They merged and sped after him, Rory and Lucas Cord in the lead.

The pinto flowed over the ground, its powerful legs driving hard, its mane flying. Fargo hunched forward and occasionally lashed the stallion with the end of the reins. They gained a few yards but they were still in rifle range. Not that the cowhands would be foolish enough to try to down him while going at an all-out gallop. It would be a waste of ammunition. Hitting a target when mounted and in motion was difficult enough; scoring at a gallop was more likely to be a fluke than the result of skill.

Gradually the hills loomed nearer. About as many were covered with trees as were barren. He made for one of those where the forest promised sanctuary from his pursuers, bearing to the left to avoid a large bunch of cattle that appeared. He was almost even with them when he spied the lone bull in his path and promptly realized he was in for trouble.

The longhorn weighed a thousand pounds or better and sported a spread of nine feet from horn tip to horn tip. Typical of the breed, it had high, thin shoulders, flat ribs, slender hips, and a back that looked like a ridgepole. It was eyeing him as it would another bull that presumed to challenge it.

Fargo tried to swing wide. Instinct told him that the brute was going to charge, and he was proven right the very next second as the longhorn broke into a lumbering run, lowered its massive head, and charged. He swung farther to the left, concerned more for the stallion than for himself. Tales of longhorn attacks were common in Texas and had spread by word of mouth to other territories, and he had heard a few during his widespread travels. He knew that a longhorn invariably went for a man's mount and tried to gore the poor horse in the stomach. If those wicked horns should rip into the pinto, the Ovaro wouldn't last out the hour.

The bull was amazingly swift.

Skye concentrated on the longhorn and nothing else. Had the pinto been an experienced cow horse, it would automatically know how to evade cattle. But he had never worked as a cowhand. Their survival depended on his horsemanship and the pinto's speed and agility. In the back of his mind he toyed with the notion of shooting the bull, although he preferred to flee rather than slay it for doing what came naturally.

Snorting, its head lowered to slash and tear, the bull closed rapidly.

Fargo intentionally slowed. He carefully gauged the distance between the pinto and the longhorn and tried not to look at those glittering horns. Then, when the bull was less than ten feet off and running too fast to stop quickly, he jammed his spurs into the Ovaro. The stallion bounded ahead. He heard the pounding of the bull's heavy hoofs and saw clods of dirt flying from under the onrushing mass of muscle, and then the longhorn swept past, its horn missing the pinto by mere inches.

Fargo made for the hills, the Ovaro at top speed. He twisted and saw the bull had stopped and was glaring after them in evident frustration. Shifting his gaze to the RC outfit, he tensed. The delay had proven costly. Cord and his men were only one hundred yards to the rear. Most had taken their rifles from their saddles.

He bent low and rode on. A shot cracked, but the cowhand wasn't much of a marksman and the slug came nowhere close. Some of the hands whooped in delight, thinking they were about to overtake him. Little did they know the Ovaro's endurance. The stallion could run for hours without tiring. Their horses, on the other hand, were accustomed to putting on short bursts of speed when needed to keep cattle in line. Seldom did they take part in a sustained chase.

More shots cracked.

Fargo hoped the Ovaro wouldn't be hit. He was within half a mile of a wooded hill, within half a mile of shelter. If only his luck would hold! Longhorns dotted the grassland before him but none showed any hostility.

Someone shouted behind him.

He risked a glance and saw Cord had ordered the riders to separate again with half bearing to the left, half to the right. What did they intend to accomplish? They certainly weren't going to stop him from attaining the trees unless the pinto should step into a prairie dog burrow, or another kind of hole or rut, and go down.

True to his prediction, Skye reached the hill. He plunged into the forest, then instantly reined up, grabbed the Sharps, and dismounted. The two groups of cowhands were eighty yards out and about thirty yards apart. They were also growing farther apart by the moment. At last he understood. They were going to flank him and spread around the base of the hill, trapping him on it. Innocent or not, he couldn't let them complete their trap.

He faced the bunch on his right, snapped the rifle to his shoulder, and cocked the hammer. Taking a steady bead on one of the formost rider's mounts, he hesitated. Under ordinary circumstances he would never slay a horse, but in this case it was either the animal or the rider and for all he knew none of Cord's men were involved in Whitman's disappearance. What choice did he have? Reluctantly, he fired.

Sixty yards off the horse went into a roll. The cowhand sailed through the air and smacked onto the ground, unconscious. His companions, fearful for their lives, swung away from the hill to get beyond rifle range.

Fargo shifted, reloaded, and aimed at the lead horse on the left. As luck would have it, the rider was Lucas Cord and Skye was strongly tempted to shoot him instead. But as with the cowhands, he had no proof Lucas had done anything to Whitman, and since he was the trespasser on Cord property the law would hold him accountable if he shot Lucas without a clear-cut excuse. Frowning, he shot the horse.

The animal went down in a whirlwind of flailing legs and tail, throwing the rest of the horses into confusion. Another animal stumbled and fell. Tugging frantically on their reins, the remaining riders brought their mounts under control and galloped to the east so they wouldn't become targets.

Fargo whirled and mounted. The ruse had worked, temporarily. Rory Cord was bound to rally his men, and he had to be long gone before the hands closed on the hill again. Up the slope he went, wending among the trunks, and on the rim he halted. The two groups had stopped, each approximately three hundred yards from the base of the hill. They were yelling back and forth. Apparently Rory wanted them to press the attack and some of the hands were refusing.

Smart men.

He was about to depart when he saw one of the riders scanning the hill with an object that gleamed in the sunlight. It took a moment for him to realize the man held a telescope. They were popular with scouts and the military, but he'd never heard of a cowhand owning one before. It made sense, though. A man could spot stray cattle easier and save a lot of saddle wear. Now he knew how they had spotted him riding up to the ranch.

Hastily, he rode down the opposite side and continued northward, staying off the high ground this time so he wouldn't silhouette himself. There were gullies and ravines everywhere, a virtual maze, but he unerringly stayed on course until he had five miles behind him. Then he rode to the top of a ridge and checked his back trail.

They were coming.

Fargo estimated they were two miles from the ridge. Evidently they had a tracker among them because one of the hands was kneeling to examine his tracks. Damn! He hadn't counted on that. Now he must work to lose them.

He descended the ridge, headed west, and came to a narrow canyon with high rock walls. Hoping it wasn't a dead end, he entered. The pinto's hoofs echoed hollowly as he progressed for a quarter of a mile. Gradually the walls narrowed until there was barely room for the stallion. He began to worry he had boxed himself in when the walls widened out again and he spied a deer trail leading to the south rim. He also saw something else of interest. Precariously balanced above the point where the walls spread out were five or six large boulders.

The Ovaro took the trail nimbly, and once on top he climbed off and walked to the edge. Rory Cord and the RC outfit were over a mile from the canyon, riding at a gallop. They were in for a little surprise. He stepped to a boulder situated at the very brink, braced his back against it, and strained with every sinew in his body. His boot heels dug into the ground, gouging furrows in the dry soil. His ribs acted up again but he bit his lower lip and bore the pain.

For quite a while nothing happened. The boulder refused to budge, and all his pushing and grunting was only making him tired. On the verge of calling it quits, he nearly fell on his backside when the boulder suddenly gave way, tilted sharply, and plunged from the summit. He recovered his balance and peered over the rim to see the boulder crash down with an impact that seemed to shake the very canyon, smack between the walls and precisely where he wanted.

He applied himself to another boulder, to one perched on a pile of rocks and dirt, and pushed as with the first. This time the task was easier. After a minute the boulder slid a few inches, then the rocks and dirt gave way and cascaded into the canyon. Lacking its foundation, the boulder hurtled over the edge and bounced off the wall twice before smashing to a rest close to the first one. Between the two boulders there was no way a horse could get through the narrow gap.

Rory Cord and the RC hands would be mad as hell.

Skye climbed on the stallion and rode due south for a mile. He realized he was close to the Bear River and went west until he reined up on its bank. The pinto could use a rest and so could he. He let the Ovaro drink, then sat down with his back against a tree while the sweaty stallion grazed on lush grass.

What had he accomplished so far? Not a thing, in his estimation. He'd learned that Rebecca Cord was basically a decent woman married to a bully. It was ironic that he owed his life to the wife of the man who wanted him dead. If she hadn't let him escape, Cord would surely have killed him. He hoped Cord wasn't the type to take out his anger by beating his wife.

His thoughts strayed to the odd remark she had made about someone being a hussy. The bitterness in her voice had been genuine. He debated whether to try and talk to her once more. Cord would likely never leave the ranch unattended again, so his best chance of getting her alone for a few minutes might be if she ever came to town.

When the Ovaro had eaten its fill and appeared well rested, Fargo forked leather and made for Beartown. He stayed in the hills until they petered out. From then on he availed himself of whatever cover was handy and kept well shy of the dirt road connecting the town to the RC ranch.

Beartown was quiet when he rode in toward evening. The stable was his first stop, and as he was rubbing the pinto down footsteps sounded and Kellerman appeared at the open end of the stall.

"Your horse is a bit tuckered out," the liveryman said.

"We've had a long day."

"Had someone in here earlier asking about you."

Fargo stopped stroking. "Who?"

"That skinny feller who fancies himself to be a bad man and works for Cord."

"Tillman?"

"I believe that's his handle. He walked in here like he owned the place and wanted to know if I was renting a stall to you and how many times a day you come by and so forth."

"What did you tell him?"

Kellerman smiled. "Same thing I told you. What happens at my establishment is my business and nobody else's. He didn't take to kindly to that and cussed me out so I gave him ten seconds to leave or be tossed out on his ear. He left."

"Thanks for letting me know," Fargo said.

"I'm not taking sides, you understand," Kellerman responded. "I don't meddle in the affairs of others. But I don't think very highly of Rory Cord and you strike me as a decent man. You know how to take care of a horse proper, and I've learned to judge a man by the way he treats his horse. There are some folks who leave their animals here and don't stop by for days. They couldn't care less if their poor critters are lonely and need tending."

Fargo was thinking of Tillman. Had the thin man been with the bunch out at the ranch? Now that he thought of it, he couldn't recall seeing him. Why had Tillman been sent into town to check on his comings and goings? What did Rory Cord have up his sleeve?

"Anyway," Kellerman was saying, "I just figured you should know." He nodded and walked off.

Skye finished the rubdown and carried his saddlebags

and the Sharps to the Whitman house. The newspaper office was deserted. "Is anyone home?" he shouted as he closed the front door, but no one replied. Maybe they were over at Ruth's, he reflected, and walked down the hallway to his room. The door hung open a few inches. He distinctly recalled leaving it closed. Placing the rifle and his saddlebags on the floor, he drew the Colt and kicked the door so that it slammed against the wall. He checked under the bed, then in the closet. All appeared safe.

His stomach rumbled to remind him that he hadn't eaten since breakfast. Eager to visit the restaurant, he deposited the Sharps and the saddlebags at the foot of the bed and turned to leave when he heard a slight rustling noise in the hall. He stepped to one side of the doorway, leveled the Colt, and waited. A floorboard in the hall creaked.

Not two seconds later one of the twins slid into the room, attired in a sheer, lacy nightgown and nothing else.

8

Skye Fargo lowered the Colt in surprise. The twin wore her hair down so he was unable to see her earlobes. But he knew which one it had to be. "Mercia?"

"You were expecting someone else?" she responded with a grin and nodded at the revolver.

"I wouldn't put anything past Cord," Skye said. He eased the .44 into his holster and moved away from the wall. "Where's Marcia? Aren't you taking a big chance that she'll see you?"

"Who cares if she does?" Mercia said, stepping up to him and posing seductively with her hands clasped behind her back and her spine arched to thrust her gorgeous breasts against the sheer material covering them. "I do as I damn well please." She snickered, then quickly closed the door. "Besides, Marcia is over at a friend's house and won't be back for hours. I've locked the front door, so it's just you and me."

"What do you have in mind?" Fargo asked, knowing full well her intentions. His meal, it seemed, would have to wait, and he resigned himself to the inevitable. It wouldn't be the first time he had his dessert before the main course.

"I can't stop thinking about last night," Mercia said, draping her arms over his shoulders. Her eyes twinkling mischievously, she licked her cherry red lips and kissed him lightly.

Skye placed his hands on her back, then ran his palms down the silken nightgown and cupped her buttocks. She giggled and wiggled against him, the heat from her mound arousing his manhood. "You weren't kidding when you said that you're the wild one," he reminded her.

75

"I like being unpredictable," she replied. As if to emphasize her point, she bit him on the chin.

Fargo involuntarily winced. She bit so hard she nearly drew blood, and when she pulled back and smirked he returned the favor, clamping his teeth down until she squealed.

"Ouch! You're hurting me!"

"That will teach you," Skye said, and kissed her. She mashed herself into him, her tongue meeting his and entwining. Her breath was hot, her skin warm. His organ shot up, pressing tight against the junction of her thighs, and she moaned deep in her throat.

All thoughts of food were forgotten as Fargo eased her to the bed and stretched out on his side next to her. Not once did she break the kiss. Her hands roved everywhere before settling at his waist and tugging his shirt free of his pants. Then he felt her fingers on his stomach, artfully kneading his flesh. One hand suddenly darted to his manhood and stroked its entire length. Now it was his turn to moan.

He hiked at her nightgown until the hem was up to her waist. Her skin was glass, her thighs exquisite. He dallied there, massaging her from her hips to her knees, delighting in the tiny quivers of her skin and the way she partially opened and closed her legs in rhythm to his strokes. She was busy running her hands over his chest and the corded muscles along his abdomen. Her breasts rose and fell with each panting breath.

Skye brought his left hand up to her matching globes and tweaked their nipples. She tossed back her head and sighed languidly, her fingernails digging into his shoulders.

"You sure know how to do it right," Mercia said.

"Practice makes perfect," Fargo responded, and lifted her garment to fasten his greedy mouth to her left breast. He nibbled lightly at the hard nipple, then worked the nipple between his lips while squeezing the breast. She arched her back and her hips pumped a few times.

Mercia was already primed to go all the way.

He transferred his mouth to her right breast and gave it the same treatment. Her knee poked between his legs and proceeded to rub him where it would do the most good, firing his lust to a fever pitch. His hand descended to her navel, then to her thatch of pubic hair, and finally into the welcoming crevice between her legs.

"Oh, yes!" Mercia cried.

Fargo was amazed at how hot and wet she was, even more so than the night before. Her slit seemed to part of its own accord and suck his forefinger into her core, and she trembled in delirious ecstasy once he started stroking. Her eyelids were hooded, her mouth formed in a delicious oval, her breasts heaving harder with each passing moment. She was the perfect picture of female lust.

He kissed her neck, her cheeks, her brow. He kissed her shoulders, her stomach, her sides. She trembled and bent her legs to allow him to kneel between them, and when he unfastened his gunbelt and pants to expose his organ she clutched at it hungrily.

"It's bigger!" she cooed. "It's bigger!"

Bigger than what? Fargo wondered. Bigger than it had been last night? He figured she was too enrapt by sheer desire to know what she was saying. Slowly, he inserted the tip of his pole into her moist sheath, then grasped her bottom and shoved to the hilt.

Mercia nearly became airborne. Her spine bent backward almost in half and her hips surged up off the bed. She crashed down, put her hands on his bottom, and rasped, "Give it to me, Skye! Make me come!"

He started a rocking motion, rolling back and forth on his knees, his manhood creating intense friction within her. She gasped and gurgled and bit him again, this time on the shoulder, and this time she drew a trickle of blood. He straightened, placed a hand on each breast, and held her down as he continued to pump to his heart's content. There was blood on her lips, his blood, and she licked it off and tried to rise.

Fargo applied enough pressure to keep her flat on her back and drove into her slit with renewed vigor. She cried out, tossing her head from side to side. Increasing the power of his strokes, he soon had her bucking wildly and could feel her inner walls contracting around his manhood. She suddenly went into a frenzy and he matched her movements, attaining his own peak and spurting madly.

"Aaaahhhhh!" Mercia wailed. "I'm there! I'm there!"

Skye grinned and rode out the wave of their mutual passion until they both tired and subsided into quiet lassitude, lying side by side. He was hungrier than ever now and his stomach growled again.

Mercia laughed. "Sounds like you're ready for seconds."

"I haven't had a bite since breakfast," he disclosed.

"Oh, yes you have," Mercia said, laughing louder and touching the spot where she had bitten his shoulder.

Skye chuckled and propped himself up on one elbow. His eyes drank in her superb beauty and lingered on her radiant face. "Does your sister know what a wildcat you are?"

"I doubt it. She actually doesn't know me very well, although she thinks she does."

He stroked her neck and she twisted to smile up at him, her hair falling away from her face. The temptation was too much to resist and he kissed her.

"So tell me," Mercia prompted when he lifted his head. "How did it go today? Any luck in learning our father's fate?"

"I'm afraid not," Skye admitted. "I rode out to the Cord ranch but all I managed to do was nearly get myself trapped and killed."

"Then you don't have a clue?"

"No."

"You're sure?"

"Of course."

"Do you know anything that would implicate the Cords?"

Fargo moved his elbow a bit to relieve a cramp in his upper arm. "If I did, you'd be the first one I'd tell." He smiled and traced his finger around her mouth. His gaze went to her right ear, then idly to her left, and he nearly leaped off the bed in his astonishment. He blinked, looked again, and averted his eyes so she wouldn't see his reaction.

The left earlobe was smaller than the right!

He told himself he must be imagining things, that the subdued light had played a trick on him. But when he checked a third time it was the same. Her left lobe was definitely smaller, which meant he hadn't just made love to Mercia.

This was Marcia!

Skye cleared his throat and sat up, his mind swirling. What the hell was Marcia trying to prove? Why had she deceived him? Since she had no idea he could tell the sisters apart, she must have felt confident she could pull off the deception. To what end? Had she decided she wanted him, but she didn't want to hurt Mercia's feelings by making a play for him herself? Was this her way of getting him in the sack without Mercia being the wiser? It didn't seem likely. All it would take was one comment from him and Mercia would know they had been to bed.

"Something wrong, honey?" she asked dreamily.

"No," Fargo lied. If he confronted her now, he might never learn her motive. Maybe if he played along for the time being, she would tip her hand later. "I'm just hungry."

"I'd offer to fix a meal for you but I have an appointment to keep in a while."

Interesting, Fargo reflected, and stood. "I can eat at Ruth's," he said. As he made himself presentable Marcia blew him a kiss and dashed out of the bedroom. He strapped on the Colt, then walked to the outer office. Upstairs a door slammed. He stepped out on the boardwalk to find Beartown shrouded in twilight and few people outside. It was the supper hour and most people were inside. Turning to the right, he went to the first alley, made certain no one was watching, and slipped from sight. Standing in the shadows, he leaned his shoulder on the corner so he could observe the house unseen.

The minutes crawled by. He gazed at the restaurant and spied Mercia and Ruth seated near the front window, involved in an animated discussion. Boot steps sounded on the boardwalk and he drew back as a pair of townsfolk went by. Neither of the men looked into the alley.

More time passed. He began to think he had made a mistake, that Marcia might leave by the rear door, and was about to go to the other end of the alley to check when the front door opened and out she came, all fresh and bright in a pretty blue dress and bonnet. She checked both ways, then hastened straight toward him.

Skye moved deeper into the shadows, his back flat to the wall, until she hurried past. Marcia was staring at the restaurant, her body posture suggesting she didn't want her sister to spot her. He waited until her footsteps told him she was at least a dozen yards off before he moved to the alley mouth to spy on her.

Marcia hugged the walls of the buildings she passed as if she didn't want anyone to see her if it could be helped. Once, close to the general store, she drew up short when a elderly woman emerged and stood stock still until the woman had gone her way without noticing Marcia was there. On she went until she was directly opposite the livery. Another quick check of the street, then she darted across to the livery entrance and vanished within.

Fargo took the opportunity to move to the next alley. He figured she was saddling a horse and wondered where she could be going so late in the day. Since she still hadn't appeared, he went to the next alley and was almost there when Marcia abruptly materialized in the entrance. He froze, expecting her to see him, but she didn't bother to look in his direction. With a flick of a quirt she brought her mount to a canter and headed west.

He watched her back until she reached the end of the main street where in a flurry of hoofs she galloped off to the north. But the only thing off in that direction was the RC ranch! Perplexed, he cut across the street to the livery. He would mount up and follow her and hopefully get to the bottom of the mystery.

A single lantern hanging from a beam at the center of the stable was the only source of light. He saw no sign of Kellerman as he ran to the pinto's stall and reached for his saddle.

Somewhere at the back of the livery someone moaned.

Instantly, Skye crouched and drew the Colt. It sounded as if the person was hurt. He listened, scarcely breathing, until the moan was repeated. It came from the far rear corner where the light didn't penetrate, in an area under the hayloft. Cocking the revolver, he glided down the aisle to the last stall, then peeked out.

There was movement under the loft. A vague figure shuffled into view, holding a hand to his head.

Kellerman! Fargo realized. And there was blood on the liveryman's forehead. He stood and started forward. Kellerman took a feeble step, stumbled, and fell flat on his face, his arms outflung. In four bounds Fargo was there, kneeling to inspect a nasty gash on the top of the man's head. Someone had struck him with a heavy object. Blood poured from the wound.

Skye rose, planning to go find the town doctor, when a faint scraping noise overhead caused him to look up just as a thin form hurtled straight at him, a form clutching a dagger and sneering in unbridled hatred. In the blink of an eye he recognized the man as Tillman, but before he could bring his Colt into play the RC hand smashed into him, bowling him over, the collision sending the Colt flying. He was knocked onto his back, his head spinning, his vision blurred. Knowing Tillman might bury that dagger in his body at any second, he scrambled to his knees in time to detect a flash of light and feel a lancing pain in his left shoulder. He had been stabbed. Pushing upright, he backpedaled and shook his head to clear his sight. Everything came suddenly into focus.

Tillman was six feet away, stalking him as a cat stalks a mouse, the dagger held at chest height, ready to slash and rend. "Now I get to pay you back for damn near kicking my face in," he snarled, and lunged.

Skye retreated, the keen blade missing him by inches. He cast about for the Colt and failed to spot it. Unfortunately the Sharps was back at the Whitman residence. He still had the Arkansas toothpick snug in its sheath on his right ankle, but if he stooped to grab it Tillman would plant that dagger in his back.

"What's the matter?" the thin man mocked him. "Yellow?" He charged again, swinging furiously.

Darting into the aisle, Fargo ducked under a sweep to the face, then dodged to the right as Tillman reversed the thrust and tried to slice open his neck. He inadvertently backed into a stall and heard the horse whinny. Somehow he must distract Tillman long enough to grab the toothpick, but how?

"You're fast, Trailsman," the cowhand said. "But not fast enough."

Fargo saw the blade lancing at his chest and sidestepped. He seized Tillman's wrist in both hands, pivoted, and swung the thin man into the end of the stall. Tillman hit with a loud thud, staggered, and tried to turn.

But Skye now had the advantage and had no intention of losing it. He leaped, catching Tillman's right wrist in his left hand to hold the dagger at bay. His other hand clamped on Tillman's neck. The thin man retaliated by seizing his throat. He could feel Tillman's fingers digging into his skin and sank his own into Tillman's. They struggled silently, fiercely, each trying to strangle the other.

Tillman broke the deadlock. He swept his right boot up into Skye's groin, then shoved when Skye's grip loosened.

Overcome by pounding waves of agony, Fargo stumbled backward, tripped, and fell. He threw himself to the side as the dagger streaked by his head, then tried to kick Tillman in the knee but the thin man nimbly skipped away. His manhood in torment, he rose into a crouch and stumbled to the nearest stall where he braced his arm for support and tried to regain his self-control.

Oddly, Tillman wasn't pressing the attack. He stood a couple of yards off, grinning in triumph while tapping the flat side of the blade on his palm. "You aren't so tough, after all. I reckon I'll carve you into little pieces and leave them for the marshal to find."

"What about Kellerman?" Fargo asked, stalling to give himself the time he needed to recover.

"Can't kill him. He's one of the townspeople and they'd have a fit if one of their own bit the dust," Tillman said, taking a stride. "But you're a stranger. No one gives a damn about you except maybe the twins and that biddy who owns the restaurant."

"What if Kellerman saw you hit him?" Fargo said, straightening with a supreme effort. His fingers brushed something hanging over the stall. Out of the corner of his eye he saw it was a bridle.

"Not a chance," Tillman responded, taking another step. "I came up on the grump from behind. He's lucky I didn't split his damn skull for the sass he gave me earlier."

Fargo shifted position so that his body blocked the sight of his right hand gripping the bridle. He grimaced to show he was still in terrible misery. "From behind? I should have known. And you have the gall to call *me* yellow!"

The insult had the desired effect. Tillman hissed like a cottonmouth and sprang, the dagger extended.

Skye was ready. Moving quickly to the left, he whipped the bridle in an overhand arc and caught the thin man flush on the face, a section of the cheek-piece lashing Tillman right across the eye. Screeching, Tillman blinked and backed off, a red welt marking his skin. Skye moved in, wielding the bridle as he would a rawhide whip, always keeping it in motion. Tillman jabbed ineffectively with the dagger, his lacerated eye watering like crazy.

"You son of a bitch!" he bellowed.

Fargo swung again. This time he telegraphed the blow by drawing his right arm back, which gave Tillman a chance to easily move aside. It was then, as Tillman was moving, that Fargo swiftly squatted, got his fingers on the toothpick, and yanked it out. He tossed the bridle to the ground. "Now we're even," he said.

The thin man didn't like the turn of events. He stared at the toothpick, then nervously licked his lips.

"Any time," Fargo said.

Tillman came on in a frenzied rush, apparently hoping to prevail through sheer brute force. His dagger weaved a glittering pattern in the air as he executed a figure eight motion over and over.

Fargo knew better than to try and meet the rush head-on. An experienced knife fighter relied more on proper timing and speed than sheer strength. He retreated before the rush and saw Tillman smile. The cowhand tried to get in closer but Fargo was always one step ahead of him. He didn't even bother to parry the dagger. He simply evaded it.

Tillman became desperate. Several times he glanced at the livery entrance as if worried someone would show up before he finished Skye off.

Or so Fargo thought until a mare near the entrance nickered and seconds later he heard someone running toward them. One of the townspeople? He steered clear of a downward swipe and shifted. Rushing at him was the cowhand named Burt, the pitchfork upraised for a death stroke. He barely had time to chide himself for not even considering that Tillman wouldn't have come into town alone, and then Burt was on him, delivering a swing designed to impale him from sternum to spine.

Skye threw himself to the right. The pitchfork fanned his face and missed his chest by a hair. Suddenly Burt, the victim of his own momentum, was six inches away and desperately trying to lift the pitchfork for another try. The Arkansas toothpick leaped as of its own accord up an in, ripping into Burt's side. The cowhand screamed, let go of the pitchfork, and began to buckle.

His muscles rippling, his body a blur, Fargo released the toothpick, grasped the pitchfork handle, and took a lightning step. He speared those wicked metal prongs into Tillman's torso just above the waist and twisted as Tillman doubled over and uttered a shrill whine. Fargo wrenched the pitchfork out, prepared to strike again. But another stab wasn't needed.

The thin man tottered, his fingers spread over the multiple punctures in his abdomen, blood and gastric juices seeping between them. He gaped at Skye, then fell to his knees. Crimson spittle flecked his mouth. "Oh, God," he wailed. "Not like this. Not like this!"

"You won't last long," Fargo noted. "I can put you out of your misery if you want."

"Go to hell!" Tillman snapped, looking like a rabid dog as the spittle dribbled over his chin. He glanced down at the pistol on his hip, glared at Skye, then clutched at the gun with slippery, gore-covered fingers.

Fargo never hesitated. Again the pitchfork cleaved the air, and this time the prongs bit deep into Tillman's head, one piercing his right eye. Tillman grunted, straightened, and pitched forward to convulse violently for half a minute before he exhaled loudly and was still.

Skye heard someone clear his throat behind him and whirled.

"It's only me," Marshal Fred Bullock said, advancing with amazement lining his fleshy features. "I saw Burt run in here and figured I'd find out why." He stared at Burt's body, then at Tillman's.

"Kellerman is in the back," Fargo informed him. "He needs a doctor. Tillman nearly caved his head in."

"I'll fetch the doc," Bullock said, turning to go. "You stay put. I want to hear all about what happened." He hesitated as if about to ask a question.

"Yes?" Skye prompted.

The marshal nodded at the corpses. "Does a day ever go by when you *don't* kill somebody?"

9

The restaurant was still open two hours later when Skye emerged from the marshal's office and wearily tramped across the quiet street. There were few customers at such a late hour. Ruth was clearing a table near the kitchen and the moment she saw him she hurried forward.

"You're a sorry sight."

"Just what I needed to hear," Skye said, taking a seat where he had a clear view of the doorway.

"I heard about Tillman and Burt. The story is all over town."

"Figures."

"Are you hungry?" she asked, her kindly eyes conveying her concern.

"Shot any elk lately? I could eat one all by my lonesome."

"I have some beefsteak and fresh green beans. Will that do?"

"Bring it on," Skye directed, and pushed the chair out so he could lean his shoulder on the wall. He was exhausted, as tired as a man could be and not keel over. He was also frustrated at being unable to follow Marcia. If Tillman and Burt hadn't interfered, he might have learned the reason for her secretive behavior. He debated whether to tell Mercia and decided against doing so. They just might be in cahoots.

Skye stretched and yawned. He'd been in the saddle at dawn, and what did he have to show for all his efforts? Not a thing. He would have accomplished just as much by staying in bed. Tomorrow he would try again and hope for a break. He closed his eyes and must have briefly dozed because the next thing he knew a plate laden with a thick steak and mountain of green beans was being placed in front of him. The delicious aroma brought him around with a start.

"Sorry," Ruth said. "Didn't mean to spook you." She touched the empty chair. "Mind if I sit a spell?"

"Not at all," Fargo said, glad for her company. The conversation would help to keep him awake and alert.

"The doc was in here a while ago. Said you'd been stabbed."

Fargo glanced down at his shoulder. Under his buckskin shirt was the bandage the doctor had hastily applied before tending to the livery owner. "I'm fine," he said.

"The doc also told me Kellerman will live but he'll be laid up for two weeks or better. Kellerman's sister will be running the livery until he's back on his feet."

"Doesn't he have a wife?" Fargo absently asked while cutting off a large piece of steak. He lifted it to his mouth and let it rest on his tongue, savoring the taste before taking his first bite.

"She'll have her hands full with their four youngsters," Ruth said. "So June—that's the sister—will watch the livery. She's done it before." Ruth paused. "June is a widow lady. Her husband was killed by Indians four years ago and she's never remarried."

Fargo chewed heartily, mentally noting that steak had to be the tastiest meat there was, far better than chicken, turkey, and ham. Whether beef or venison, give him a sizzling steak any time over stringy meat from ungainly birds that spent their days pecking at insects and taking dust baths, or from sweaty hogs and pigs that ate slop and wallowed in mud.

"Mercia was in here earlier," Ruth mentioned. "But I haven't seen hide nor hair of Marcia."

"What did you two talk about?"

"Mainly how much she misses her father and hopes you can discover his fate," Ruth related. "She was always closer to Adam than Marcia and I think his disappearance has hit her harder. If she was a man she'd ride out to the RC ranch all by herself and prod Cord into telling the truth, or else."

Fargo was about to fork more steak into his mouth when an important question occurred to him. "What can you tell me about Marcia? I don't know her that well."

"She's difficult to read. She rarely lets her feelings

show and she never talks about personal matters." Ruth paused. "Although there were a few times I saw her angry, usually when she was arguing with her father."

"They argued a lot?"

"Oh, I wouldn't call it a lot. But every so often I'd see them on the street spatting like two wet cats."

"What about?" Fargo probed, the steak temporarily forgotten.

"I was never close enough to hear," Ruth said. "And neither of them volunteered any information. Even Mercia didn't know. She commented once on how her father sometimes kept secrets from her. She knew Marcia and him didn't see eye to eye on something, but neither would confide in her. It hurt her feelings."

How interesting, Fargo reflected. But did it have a bearing on Whitman vanishing? A thought struck him then, a crazy idea he almost dismissed as too preposterous to be worthy of serious consideration. Given Marcia's odd behavior, though, it deserved study. Was it possible Mercia and the marshal and everyone else were wrong? Maybe the Cords were innocent, maybe they had nothing to do with whatever happened to Adam Whitman. Maybe Marcia was somehow responsible.

"Is something wrong?" Ruth asked.

"No. I'm fine," Fargo said, stuffing more steak into his mouth. She got up when a customer beckoned, leaving him to finish his meal in silence. Twice he heard a horse moving down the street and looked out the window to see townspeople going by. If there were more cowhands in Beartown they were keeping a low profile.

He paid for the meal and headed for the Whitman place, scanning the street in both directions before he ventured across. There were two men going from one saloon to another, and Marshal Bullock was standing in front of his office. Bullock gave a little wave when he spied Skye.

Mercia was working in the office when he entered. She glanced up from the pile of papers on the desk, beamed, and stood. "It's you! Where have you been? I checked your room and saw your rifle and saddlebags, so I knew you were back."

"Haven't you heard about the livery?" Fargo responded.

"No. I've been working here for hours. What happened?"

So Fargo told her, every detail except his talk with Ruth about Marcia. Mercia uttered a very unladylike curse when he was done and smacked her left fist into her right palm.

"Now we have all the proof we need that the Cords had something to do with my father disappearing," she declared. "Why else would Rory send Tillman and Burt to kill you unless the Cords are worried you'll uncover their secret?"

"Bullock sent a man out to their ranch to tell them to come into town tomorrow. He wants to question them."

"The marshal is wasting his time. They'll never admit a thing to him. Why should they? So far they've been one step ahead of everyone else."

Fargo moved closer to her and gave the office a cursory survey. "Where's your sister?"

"I don't know," Mercia answered. "Maybe she went off riding again. She does that a lot. Ever since we were little she's liked to go off on long moonlit rides. Father didn't approve and was always stopping her. She'd get mad as hell."

Could the answer be so simple? Fargo wondered. He sighed and squeezed her arm. "I'm off to bed. I need to be up early again."

"Care for some company?" Mercia asked, sidling up to him and rubbing her leg against his.

"Another time," Fargo said. He almost laughed at her crestfallen expression. Women were peculiar that way. They'd keep a man at arm's length until they were good and ready to make love to him, but once they did they acted as if they owned him and felt they had the right to rip his pants off whenever they were in the mood. If the man was brash enough to say no, they took it as a personal insult.

"You must *really* be tired," Mercia said.

"I am," Fargo replied. He headed for the hallway, his legs leaden, then paused. "Is the back door locked?"

"I don't think so."

"Lock it so none of Cord's men can pay us a visit in the middle of the night."

"Will do."

Once in his bedroom he didn't bother to turn on the lantern. He spread out on his back, set his hat beside him, and drew the Colt. With the reassuring feel of the revolver in his hand, he stared at the inky ceiling and tried to put the pieces of the puzzle together. Long before he arrived at any firm conclusions, he was sound asleep.

Both twins were busy in the kitchen when Skye entered the next morning well before six o'clock. After his undisturbed rest he felt invigorated and ravenous. Mercia was preparing batter for flapjacks while Marcia placed plates and glasses on the table.

"Sleep well?" Mercia asked.

"Never better," Fargo admitted, taking a seat. "I can't wait to hit the trail. Maybe I'll have better luck today." He looked at Marcia, keeping his features as blank as his best poker face. "Have a nice ride last night?"

Marcia paused, a spoon in her hand. "You saw me leave?"

"You weren't here when I got back and your sister told me you like to take nighttime rides. If I'd seen you leaving I would have stopped you," Fargo fibbed. "It's too dangerous for you to be out by yourself. What if the Cords found you?"

"They wouldn't hurt me," Marcia said. "They know every man in town would be out to string them up if they did."

"You're still taking a big risk. You'd be wise to stick close to home until this is settled."

Marcia slapped down the spoon. "I appreciate your concern, but I'm a grown woman and will do as I damn well please."

"Marcia!" her sister said. "He's only trying to be helpful. Why are you getting so angry?"

"I'm not."

Breakfast was conducted in an awkward silence. Marcia, despite her protest, was sullen and moody. Mercia acted bewildered by her twin's actions and dawdled over her flapjacks until Marcia left.

"I don't know what to make of her lately," Mercia said. "For once I can't tell what she's thinking. It's as if she's blocking her thoughts off from me." She seemed on the verge of tears. "Perhaps it's the strain. I haven't been myself lately, either."

"She'll come around," Fargo predicted, only to soothe Mercia's feelings. He polished off his cup of coffee and rose. "See you later." Going to his room, he retrieved the Sharps and his saddlebags.

The street was deserted. A light on in the restaurant showed Ruth getting ready for her breakfast trade. The owner of Nuckoll's General Store was sweeping off the boardwalk in front of his business. And, to Fargo's surprise, Marshal Fred Bullock stood outside the livery, his pudgy thumbs hooked in his belt.

"You need to see me?" Skye asked.

"Just wanted to make sure you're leaving town for the day like you told me you would last night," Bullock said. "With the Cords coming in, I'll be a lot happier knowing you're not around to get them riled."

"Rest easy, Marshal," Fargo said, and went into the livery. He was almost to the stall containing the Ovaro when he saw someone up in the hayloft forking hay down to the floor, and halted in surprise. A dark-haired woman of thirty or so, dressed in jeans and a flannel shirt, smiled down at him.

"Hello. You must be the one I've heard so much about, the Trailsman."

"And you must be June, Kellerman's sister," Fargo said. "I'm sorry about your brother."

"Don't be. He says it wasn't your fault. The Cords are the ones to blame," June said gruffly, lifting her hand to sweep her bangs out of her brown eyes. Her skin was tanned bronze and she had a healthy glow about her typical of those who spent a lot of time outdoors. "I fed your pinto a while ago so he should be all set to go."

"Thanks," Fargo replied, stepping into the stall.

June dropped the pitchfork and came down the ladder. "Nice horse you've got there," she complimented him as she strolled over. "We don't see too many Ovaros in these parts. Ever think of selling him?"

"I'd sooner sell an arm or a leg."

She watched him get ready. "Hope you don't mind having a woman look after him. Some of the fellers don't cotton to the idea of a woman doing a man's work, but

I'm the only one my brother can count on when he's laid up."

"I don't mind at all," Fargo said.

"Good." June grinned self-consciously and gestured at herself. "Don't mind the clothes, either. Stable work can be messy and I don't want to ruin any of the few dresses I own. So I put on these duds."

"I can still tell you're a woman."

She blushed scarlet and developed an inordinate interest in a beam overhead. "Yeah, well, most men hereabouts don't seem to notice. Maybe it's my being a widow. They don't like used merchandise."

Fargo, in the act of tightening the cinch, glanced at her. "Used merchandise can be better than new because it doesn't need to be broke in." He tapped his saddle. "Any fool knows a used saddle is more comfortable than a new one. I like used things, myself."

June patted the stallion on the rump. "My brother is right. You are a man who knows his way around." She bit her lower lip, then said quickly, "Would you be interested in having supper with me sometime? I'm a good cook if I do say so myself."

"When?"

"How about tonight. Whenever you get back. I live in a small house just south of town. Take the road at the west end of Main Street and you can't miss it."

"I'll be there," Fargo said, and smiled when she grinned like a little girl who had just been given her heart's desire.

"You won't regret coming," June said. She spun and hurried back to the loft, humming softly.

Fargo slid the Sharps into its scabbard, tied the saddlebags on, and led the stallion from the livery. Bullock was still there, leaning on the door and smirking. "You have something to say?" Fargo asked.

"No, sir. Not me," Bullock replied, then glanced into the stable and shook his head in amazement. "Although I will admit to being impressed. June always keeps to herself and seldom gives me the time of day. You come along and in five seconds have her eating out of your hand. How do you do it, if you don't mind my asking?"

"I seldom eat ham," Fargo answered, and swung up, ignoring the lawman's confounded expression. "Be seeing you," he said, riding off before Bullock could question him further. He looked forward to the meal at June's. The change would do him some good. Then, too, he didn't want to hang around the Whitman house too much or Marcia might suspect he knew something and was keeping an eye on her.

He swung northwest once Beartown fell to the rear, making for the hills bordering Bear River. With the Cords coming into town, it was best for him to avoid the road. He had no set plan. Whatever happened, happened. He would simply scour the RC range and keep his fingers crossed.

By noon he was in the low hills west of the valley. He followed the ravines and gullies down lower, sticking to the heavy brush when possible, always on the lookout for RC hands. Cattle were everywhere. He had been wrong about all the longhorns preferring the open range. There were hundreds in the brush, many bulls that regarded him as a threat and stood their ground when he approached. He wisely avoided each and every one. Thankfully, none saw fit to charge.

Repeatedly Skye wondered if he wasn't wasting his time. Finding a clue to the fate of Adam Whitman would be like finding a needle in a haystack. Search as he may, he could find no evidence of old tracks left by a single horse. He knew that even if he did find some, there was a strong likelihood the tracks would have been made by RC cowhands.

By the middle of the afternoon he was ready to return to Beartown. A dry wash appeared and he decided to check it before stopping for the day. As usual there were no horse tracks. He went over twenty yards, then drew rein on spying an animal carcass. It was a dead cow. The shredded hide and crushed neck bones told him a mountain lion had been responsible.

He started to wheel the pinto when he saw a brand on the inside of a section of hide lying nearby. It was an unmistakable LT, not an RC as it should be. Curious, he slid from the saddle and walked to the remains for a closer inspection. Vague memories stirred. He recalled hearing of an LT outfit down in Texas, one of the biggest outfits in the whole state. What was one of their cows doing there? Had Cord bought the cattle he stocked his ranch with from the LT?

Skye mounted and reversed direction. He deliberately sought out longhorns and found a bunch four hundred yards off. There was one big old bull and a dozen cows. The bull moved off twenty yards, then stopped and watched. None of the cows reacted to his approach, and he rode right up to one of them and leaned down to examine her brand. There it was, plain as day, the RC. But on closer examination he noticed the bottom of the *C* was straighter than it should be. He wasn't an expert, but it appeared as if there was another brand under the RC and the original brand had been skillfully changed.

It could only mean one thing.

Straightening, he spent the next half an hour examining two dozen head. The cattle under two years of age all bore distinct RC brands. But those over that age had clearly worn another brand at one time. He rode to the top of a hill, stared off at the distant ranch, and pondered the implications. Distracted, he failed to stay alert and realized his error when he heard the metallic click of a gun hammer being pulled back.

Instantly Fargo dived from the saddle, going to the right and drawing as he fell. A rifle boomed, the Ovaro whinnied, and he hit the hard ground on his shoulder. In a smooth backward roll he came up on one knee and saw a lone cowhand on foot fifteen yards off. The man was already ejecting the spent round. Fargo aimed and fired, the Colt bucking in his hand.

Slapped sideways, the cowhand dropped his rifle and clutched at his left shoulder. His left hand stabbed in a cross draw for a pistol on his right hip.

"I wouldn't if I were you," Fargo warned, taking a bead on the man's forehead to stress his point.

The hand hesitated, his fingers nearly touching his gun. His common sense wrestled with the impulse to kill and his common sense won. The fingers relaxed. He lifted his arm.

Rising, Fargo walked forward. Anger flooded through him, not so much over this latest attempt on his life as because of his own stupidity. "And here I figured all you cowhands were innocent," he growled.

"What are you talking about?" the man responded, lowering his right hand so he could see the bullet hole.

"You're nothing but a bunch of rustlers," Fargo snapped, halting at arm's length from the would-be killer. "I know all about the brands."

"I don't know what you mean."

"Like hell you don't," Fargo said, and lashed out, striking the man's wound with the barrel of the Colt. The cowhand's knees sagged and he grimaced in agony, then clamped a protective hand over the gun wound and glanced up.

"You had no call to do that!"

"Tell me who changed the brands," Fargo demanded.

"Go to—," the man began.

Fargo hit him again, with more force, the barrel slashing down onto the fingers spread over the bullet hole. A knuckle cracked loudly and the man screeched.

"You broke my finger!"

"And I'll keep on breaking bones until you tell me the truth," Fargo warned. "Now who changed the brands?"

Genuine worry lurked in the depths of the cowhand's eyes as he stared at the Colt. "Rory Cord will have my head if I talk. If not him, then Lucas."

"And what do you think I'll do if you don't?"

The man weighed the consequences and took a deep breath. "All right. I'll tell you if you agree to let me go. I give you my word I'll ride straight to Beartown, get doctored up, then head for parts unknown. It will be a day or two before Cord knows for sure that I've lit out and I'll need the time to get as far as I can." He paused. "Please, mister. He really will kill me."

Fargo nodded. The request was reasonable. And confirming the truth in exchange for a man's life was a fair bargain.

"Rory Cord had the brands changed," the man now said. "Did a lot of the changing himself. Others helped. Tillman, for one. Burt and Clem, too."

"You?"

"No, sir. About half the hands were in on the original roundup down in Texas. I was hired on the trail. Sure, I figured out what was going on but I never reported it to the law." He stopped and winced. "I needed the job."

"So as far as you know all the cattle Cord brought up from Texas were stolen?"

The cowhand nodded. "From what I've learned, Cord and his men ranged all over Texas, riding at night and taking a few head from each spread until he had a large enough herd to start his own outfit."

Skye had to hand it to Rory Cord. The scheme was clever. By only taking a few head from each ranch, Cord had avoided arousing suspicions of the ranchers who would chalk up the losses to predators or other causes. Now all Cord had to do was wait and let the natural increase of his stolen herd eventually make him rich as he sold only cattle bearing a legitimate RC brand to the army and points east.

"There were no hitches at all until that Whitman character had a big argument with Cord," the cowhand said, and frowned. "Then Whitman up and vanished and you had to go and get involved. You're one tough hombre, mister."

Fargo ignored the compliment. "What happened to Adam Whitman?"

"I don't rightly know," the man said, and hastily added when Skye's features became flinty, "Honest I don't! He was caught a few times snooping around the ranch and run off. Why he kept coming back, I don't know. Next thing I hear, he's disappeared and some folks in town are claiming the Cords had something to do with it. Maybe they did. I can't say."

The man seemed sincere. Fargo leaned closer, grabbed his pistol, and tossed it into a patch of weeds. At the bottom of the hill, standing among some trees, waited the cowhand's ground-hitched mount. He pointed at the horse. "I expect you to be long gone from this territory by sunup."

With an angry glance at the weeds, the cowhand turned and hurried down the slope.

Fargo slid the Colt into its holster and stepped to the Ovaro. Grabbing the Sharps, he covered the hand as the man descended to the horse. A minute later the only reminder of the cowhand's presence was a lingering trail of dust in the air. Fargo climbed into the saddle and headed south, intending to trail the man and make certain he went to Beartown and not to the Cord ranch.

After that was a supper appointment to keep. Then there was the matter of a little talk with the marshal. Rory Cord, although he didn't know it yet, was in for a nasty surprise.

Things were looking up.

Almost to the bottom of the hill, Fargo received a surprise of his own when a gunshot cracked from the direction the cowhand had taken. Expecting the worst, the Sharps in his left hand, he galloped between a pair of hills, bearing to the right to conform to the lay of the land. He crossed a shallow gully and drew rein when he spied the sprawled body of the cowhand a dozen yards away. The man's horse had drifted a short distance to the east.

Exercising caution, Fargo slid to the ground and cocked the rifle. The assassin might still be nearby. He moved to a boulder and crouched, scanning the hills on both sides, the likely places for an ambusher to pick. Not so much as a wisp of gunsmoke betrayed the murderer's location.

The cowhand groaned.

Skye reluctantly moved into the open, listening for the sound of driving hoofs that would tell him the ambusher was fleeing. A deathly silence mocked his ears. He dashed toward the cowhand to see if there was anything he could do, covering ten yards without mishap. Then, from on top of the hill on his left, a rifle spoke and the dirt in front of him sprayed onto his boots. He threw himself flat and rolled, yards from any cover.

The ambusher opened up again.

10

Skye Fargo was as exposed and helpless as a clay target at a shooting gallery. He rolled again, then again, and listened to bullets smack into the earth close to his head. A hasty glance showed him the silhouette of a head and shoulders on the rim of the hill, and he instantly wedged the stock against his right shoulder and fired. He would have been surprised if the rushed shot scored, but it did serve the purpose of making the ambusher duck from sight for a second.

Which was all Skye needed to rise and race for a patch of greasewood brush. He launched into a running leap as the killer on the hill cut loose once more. Something nipped at the heel of his boot. Then he crashed down in the center of the brush, scratching his face and hands and almost poking his eye on a tapered branch.

He knelt, reloaded, and swept the hill. The silhouette had vanished. Was the ambusher shifting positions or had he truly departed? The answer came in the faint drum of hoofbeats going in the direction of the ranch. Standing, he cautiously approached the cowhand, vigilant in case there was another rifleman in the vicinity. No shots rent the air, no one else appeared. A ragged hole and a spreading red stain on the back of the cowhand's shirt marked the exit wound made by the slug as it burst from his body. Apparently the ambusher had shot the man squarely in the chest.

Fargo knelt and touched the cowhand's shoulder. The man groaned. Skye slowly rolled him over, trying not to jar him. More blood coated the front of the shirt. The cowhand's eyelids fluttered, then snapped open. His lips twitched, widened, and formed words.

"Am I done for?"

Skye hesitated, tempted to lie. But what good would

it do to give the man false hope? Telling the truth would give him time to make peace with his Maker if he was so inclined. "Afraid so," he confirmed.

The cowhand swallowed, his Adam's apple bobbing. "I reckon my life has caught up with me. Should have stayed on the straight and narrow."

"Is there anyone you want told?"

"I don't have no close kin," the man said, and coughed. He trembled, then recovered. "Did you get him? Did you get Lucas Cord?"

"Was that who shot you?"

The man gave a weak nod.

"He got away. But I promise you he'll pay."

The cowhand gazed into Fargo's eyes. "You're a decent man, mister. Sorry I tried to kill you." His eyelids fluttered again, he inhaled noisily, and was still.

Skye suddenly realized he didn't know the man's name. He rummaged through every pocket but found no identification. Standing, he brought the Ovaro closer, then busied himself scraping out a shallow grave with a large flat rock. He dragged the body over, being careful not to smear blood on his hands or clothes, and constructed a mound of rocks to keep off the scavengers. It wasn't much but it would have to do.

He mounted, retrieved the man's horse, and headed for town. The day was almost done and once again he was no closer to solving the mystery of Adam Whitman's disappearance than he had been the day he rode into Beartown. Well, maybe a bit closer. He felt certain the Cords were responsible, but proving their guilt would be difficult. They were not the type to leave many clues to their activities.

The sun had set by the time he rode into Beartown. He went to the livery first and put up the horses. There was no sign of June, who was probably at her house waiting for him. She would have to wait a while longer. He walked to the marshal's office but Bullock was gone. So he either hung around until Bullock showed up or he ate a home-cooked meal first and notified the marshal later. His empty stomach settled the issue.

It was a calm night with a whisper of a breeze and Skye decided to walk. He held the Sharps in the crook of his left elbow and strolled to the end of Main Street, then hiked south as June had directed. Her house was easy to find, a small frame structure that could use a coat of paint and a few repairs, judging by the sagging porch overhang and a cracked post. He knocked on the door twice, then waited.

Bright light framed the doorway when June appeared, bathing her in a golden glow and enhancing the remarkable transformation that had occurred. She now wore a fetching yellow dress, a striking contrast to the lustrous black hair that fell past her slender shoulders. Her face lit up as she grasped his right hand and pulled him inside. "Thank goodness!" she exclaimed. "I was becoming worried you had changed your mind."

"Took me longer than I figured," Skye said, surveying the plainly furnished room. The carpet was threadbare, the furniture old and covered with nicks and scratches. Curtains on the window consisted of strips of faded gingham. He realized she must be pathetically poor and knew why she leaped at the chance to fill in at the livery for her brother. As with most single women trying to make a go of it, and being a widow to boot, she must have an extremely hard time making ends meet.

June noticed his survey. "It's not exactly a palace," she said, frowning. "But it's all my husband left me. We didn't have much in the way of savings."

"You have a nice home," Fargo told her, and was rewarded with a grateful smile.

"Let me take your gun," June said. She leaned the Sharps against the wall, then ushered him to the best chair on the premises. "Would you care for a drink? Whiskey is all I have. I never touch the stuff myself, but my husband liked to take a nip now and then."

"Whiskey will be fine," Fargo said, and watched her go to a cupboard. The pretty dress clung to her attractive figure. Her shapely hips swayed as she moved while her large breasts jiggled temptingly. It amazed him that no one had come along after her husband died to court her. Women were scarce west of the Mississippi, and an attractive woman like June usually had more suitors than they knew what to do with.

"Do you use your maiden name now?" he asked as she poured his drink.

"No, I still use my married name. June Abernathy."

"Have any other relatives besides your brother?"

"A sister in New Orleans. She wants me to come live with her, claims the frontier is no place for a lone woman." June brought the glass over.

"Why not take her up on the offer?"

"Because I won't be a burden to her or anyone else, and if I went there I'd have to live with her family. I couldn't afford a place of my own and I have no guarantee I could find work."

Skye sipped at the whiskey and found it excellent. "You could always sell your house," he commented.

June gazed fondly at the shabby furnishings. "I know. But I can't bring myself to do it yet. Bill and I were so happy here. We never had much. We usually lived hand to mouth. But we were so very happy."

"Any man in his right mind would be happy with you as his wife," Fargo said, smiling when she blushed exactly as she had that morning. "And I think it's only fair that I let you know I'm not the marrying kind. I'm just not ready and may never be."

"Understood," June said, gently placing her warm hand on his. "Now you sit there and enjoy your drink while I set supper on the table." She squeezed his hand and went through a doorway on the left.

Skye leaned back, closed his eyes, and truly relaxed for the first time that day. Unless Marshal Bullock was the gabby sort, no one else knew he would spend the evening at June's. Certainly none of the Cord outfit knew, so there was no need to worry about being shot at again. He could enjoy June's company and temporarily forget about his problems.

When she called him to the table he was surprised to find a feast fit for a cattle baron, with beef, potatoes and gravy, corn, and bread baked that very day. He guessed she had spent a lot of her meager pocket money just to please him and felt guilty at her going overboard on his account. "You shouldn't have," he said.

"No man walks away from my table with an empty stomach," June responded. "Since I haven't had the company of a man in quite a spell, and since I don't often eat such a fancy meal, I figured I'd treat both of us."

The food, true to her boast, was superb. Fargo ate

heartily, knowing to do otherwise would hurt her feelings. A second and third helping of everything sufficed to fill him up, and at the end of the meal she brought in a steaming pot of coffee and apple pie. Suddenly he found more room in his stomach. She grinned at him as he polished off half of the pie and downed four cups of coffee.

"I gather you were hungry," she joked.

"It was a long day," Fargo said.

"My Bill had a healthy appetite, too," June said, "but he was no match for you."

They repaired to the worn sofa. Fargo politely sat down at one end and was taken aback when she practically sat in his lap. Her shoulder brushed his, her legs were an inch away. She offered a shy smile and folded her hands in her lap. The conflicting cues puzzled him, but taking a cue from her forward behavior he draped his right arm across her shoulders.

June started, then blushed yet again and coughed. "Sorry. I'm not accustomed to having a man in the house. There's only been one other I've dated since Bill died and that didn't work out."

"Anyone I know?" Fargo asked merely to hold up his end of the conversation.

"Lucas Cord."

For a second Fargo thought her humor was in very poor taste, until he realized she was serious. Her face was somber when he looked at her and she met his gaze with steady eyes. "I've had a few run-ins with the Cords," he mentioned.

"So I've heard," June said. "Which is part of the reason I brought up his name. When Lucas first came to Beartown he flattered me with a lot of attention. Later I learned he was only interested in one thing."

"Oh."

"I found out the hard way when he took up with someone else," June went on. "And I wouldn't have learned about her if she hadn't come to my house and told me in no uncertain terms to stay away from him or she would see that I joined my husband in the grave."

"This other woman said *that*?"

"And other things no lady would repeat in front of a gentleman," June replied. "She needn't have worried.

Once I found out Lucas was playing me for a fool I wanted nothing to do with him. Every so often he rides out this way and tries to sweet talk me into forgiving him, but I won't."

"Good for you," Fargo said. He saw her give him an odd glance and open her mouth as if to say something. Instead, she closed it and bowed her head. "You deserve better than him. One day a man like your Bill will come along."

"My sister thinks I'd have a better chance of finding a new husband in New Orleans," June said, then added in a rush of words, "If you kill Lucas, I won't mind."

What was he supposed to say to something like that? Skye asked himself. And why had she brought it up? "It might just come to that. Lucas tried to shoot me today. The first chance I get I aim to return the favor."

June lapsed into silence, nervously rubbing her fingers together.

At a loss to know what she expected of him, Fargo said, "If you want me to go, I will."

For an answer, June turned, clamped both hands on his temples, and pulled his face down to hers. She pressed her full lips against his mouth, her tongue flicking out to probe between his parted teeth. Her fingers entwined in his hair, caressed his ears. When she pulled back she was breathing heavily.

"What was that for?" Fargo asked.

"Need you ask?" June rejoined, and suddenly sculpted her soft body to his hard one while showering tiny kisses on his cheeks and neck. Her hands molded his chest and stomach as if she were molding clay. Several times she mewed like a kitten.

Fargo had the impression she was trying to climb into his body and he had no intention of stopping her. June tugged at his shirt, hiked it above his belt, and plunged her hot hands underneath to rub his skin. She sucked on his earlobe, then bit him on the shoulder. His desire climbed, as did his manhood, and when she reached down to grab hold of him he thought he would spurt in his pants.

He became aggressive himself, bending her head back to kiss her while placing his right hand on her breast. She squirmed, panting into his mouth, her mews changing to outright groans. He squeezed her breast, causing her to shudder, triggering an unexpected reaction.

June became a tigress. Where he had been ravenous for food, she was ravenous for his body, for the intimate sharing between a man and a woman so long denied her. Her hands massaged his chest and his back, her legs rubbed his nonstop. His roving fingers touched her nether mound, eliciting a strangled cry.

Fargo became as hot as a burning log. Her passionate heat drove up his own temperature, driving him to strip off his shirt and gunbelt. He eagerly unfastened her dress, pulled the top down to her waist, and admired her ripe globes as they heaved with each breath she took. His lips found her right nipple, his tongue lashing it back and forth.

"It's been so long, so very long," June whispered. "Do with me as you please."

Such an appealing invitation was irresistible. Fargo eased her onto her back and stretched out beside her. There was barely enough room for both of them; he had to keep one foot braced on the floor to keep from falling off. He cupped her gorgeous left breast, his thumb swirling her large nipple. His mouth descended on her other breast. Between the thumb and the mouth he had her thrashing and moaning in no time.

He parted her underclothes to gain access to her womanly delights. She opened her legs to receive his hand, her slitted eyes fogged with lust. His fingers crept to her nether lips, and the moment he touched her silken portal she pumped her hips wildly.

"Oh, oh, oh!" June cried. "I've been thinking of you all day. Dreaming of you and me."

Lonely women, Fargo reflected, often made the best lovers. His finger glided into her moist womanhood, all the way to the knuckle, setting off earthquake tremors deep within her. Her walls contracted, encasing his finger. The tip of her tongue protruded between her lips as she closed her eyes and tossed her head from side to side.

He put two fingers inside her and she came up off the sofa as if trying to fly. Her sex was an inferno, her skin flushed pink. She pulled his mouth to hers, her lips melting into his, her tongue chasing his all over, He aligned himself between her willowy legs, then loosened his pants so his pole could spring free. She eagerly clutched at it and guided the tip to the entrance of her core.

Skye removed his two fingers, slowly penetrated her womanhood, then buried his organ. She trembled violently and clasped her sinuous arms around him, bucking to meet the tempo of his initial thrusts. Theirs was a fiery consummation brought on by the red hot fever of her desire and their mutual attraction. He pounded and pounded, listening to the smacking of their bellies and the squeals of joy she uttered.

June went stiff for a moment, then bucked frantically. "Now, Skye! Make it now!"

He had no trouble complying with her request. The familiar tingle of sheer ecstasy rippled from the base of his spine, through his hips, and coursed along his organ. The explosion staggered him, making him arch his back and snarl like a mating wolf. He sprayed her insides and felt them quiver.

Later, after they coasted to a weary collapse and he lay quiet on top of her, she ran her fingers through his hair and chuckled.

"What's so funny?" Skye asked.

"You've lost your hat somewhere."

"I seem to be making a habit of losing it lately," he admitted, and then hoped she wouldn't take the comment the wrong way and become offended. Her next remark put his worry to rest.

"You're welcome to lose it at my place any time you want," June said.

"I may just take you up on you generous offer," Skye said. He pecked her ear and shifted his weight so as not to crush her. His hand idly stroked her side.

"Skye?"

"What is it?"

"There's something I've been meaning to tell you, something I think you should know. I'm the only one who does so far."

"So tell me," Fargo said dreamily, starting to succumb to an impulse to doze.

"It's about Lucas Cord."

He was all attention in an instant. "Go on."

"Remember I told you Lucas took up with another

woman and I wouldn't have anything to do with him after that?"

"Yes," Fargo said, feeling his body involuntarily tense ever so slightly as if in the recesses of his mind he knew what she was going to say before she spoke.

"The woman he took up with was Marcia Whitman."

11

A myriad of stars sparkled in the firmament when Skye Fargo made his weary way into Beartown. A chill north-westerly breeze helped keep him alert. After two bouts of intense lovemaking with June Abernathy, he needed all the help he could get. She had drained him dry, sucked the life from his limbs with her insatiable sexual appetite.

Beartown was dead. Not a soul stirred on any of the streets. The marshal's office was dark, the saloons closed. Empty hitching posts would have to await the dawn before horses would again be tied to them.

He walked down the center of the deserted main street rather than use the boardwalk and have his boots clump noisily and possibly disturb the slumber of a restless townsman. The livery door hung open. Since he had promised June he would close it for the night, he angled across the street, the Sharps cradled in his arms.

In the stillness even the faintest sounds carried far. So it was that Fargo heard the scrape of a boot heel in the alley flanking the livery in time to throw himself to the ground before a revolver spat flame and lead. There was no conscious reasoning on his part. He automatically knew that none of Beartown's upstanding citizens would be lurking in an alley in the middle of the night. Nor would Bullock be waiting there to see him. Any drunks who hadn't made it home would be soundly sleeping off their binge. If someone moved back there, it could only mean one thing. And he was right.

He landed on his stomach, hastily sighted the Sharps, and got off a thundering shot as the gunman fired twice more and two small geysers of dirt flew into his face. Shoving upright, he dashed for the open livery doors and made it inside as a rifle across the street boomed. The slug clipped the fringe on his shirt.

There was more than one!

Skye rounded the corner of a stall and crouched. They had him trapped, and to make matters worse a solitary lantern glowed not ten feet away. He drew the Colt and shot it out, then leaned the Sharps on the stall and waited. The bushwhackers had to be from the RC spread, and they had to know that the marshal and every man in Beartown would come on the run. They must finish him off quickly.

Boots pounded. A shadowy form darted into the livery, slanting to the right toward the other row of stalls.

Fargo pointed the Colt at the center of the form and squeezed off a shot. The cowhand—or, more rightly, rustler—snapped off a shot of his own, enabling Fargo to peg his position and return fire so swiftly the two shots blended into one. A heavy thud confirmed his slug had hit home.

There was a loud gurgling, then a quavering voice pleaded, "Help me! Oh, God! I'm dyin'."

Skye had no intention of moving. The other rustler was out there somewhere, possibly moving toward the livery. He pressed his body close to the stall, hearing yells erupt along Main Street as men and women who had been roused from sleep by the shots demanded to know what was going on. Soon the bravest would venture out to investigate. Soon the marshal would appear. The rifleman must make his move in the next minute or give up the attempt.

A rustling noise came from the back of the livery.

Twisting, Skye probed the darkness and mentally berated himself for being a jackass and not figuring on the rifleman running all the way around to the rear of the stable. Or was it yet another RC hand? Now he had to spot the killer before the killer spotted him.

He watched the Ovaro. The stallion was gazing at the back of the stable, its ears pricked. Ordinarily wary of strangers, it was intently watching the intruder, turning its head as the man moved slowly forward. Although Skye couldn't see the pinto's eyes, he could tell by the position of its head the general direction of the killer.

The man was on his side of the aisle, advancing at a snail's pace.

From a block or two down the street arose a bellow. "I think the shots came from the livery!"

"Where's the marshal?" someone responded.

Fargo took a calculated gamble. He didn't want the rifleman to flee and try to kill him another day. He had to make certain the man was disposed of right then and there. So he suddenly threw himself into the aisle, onto his right shoulder, his arm extended and the Colt cocked. The rifleman detected the movement and fired twice, his slugs cleaving the air at waist height. Skye squeezed off two shots of his own, aiming at where he judged the rifleman's chest to be.

A loud crash attended the shots, a horse whinnied, and something thumped onto the ground.

Fargo heard footsteps outside. He rose to his knees as light flooded the interior. Framed in the opening was Marshal Fred Bullock, barefoot and wearing just his undershirt and pants, a revolver in his right hand. Behind the lawman other townsmen appeared, some with lanterns, all craning their necks to see the bodies.

Bullock stepped inside, glancing at the cowhand near the entrance who was moaning feebly, then at the prone figure farther down the aisle. He looked at Skye. "What is it with you? Every time you go near a livery stable someone tries to kill you."

"They're more of Cord's men," Fargo said, rising.

"I know," Bullock said. He tucked his pistol under his waistband and addressed the crowd at the door. "Someone fetch the doc. Tell him to come quick. Somebody else get the undertaker. The rest of you go back to your beds."

A couple of men instantly ran off and most of the onlookers dispersed. Several, however, lingered.

"How much longer do we have to put up with this, Marshal?" a white-haired man in a red nightshirt demanded. "As law-abiding citizens we shouldn't have to put up with this gunfighting at all hours of the day or night. Sooner or later a bystander is going to be wounded or worse, and you know it as well as I do."

"No one wants it stopped more than me, Fred," Bullock said.

"Then why aren't you doing something about it?" the irate citizen inquired.

"Yeah," threw in another man, glaring at Skye. "We never had any problem until this Trailsman character came along. Throw him out of town and tell him to never come back."

"I'll take your advice into consideration, Ernest," the marshal said. "Now get home before your wife starts to worry. All of you."

"We'll go," the white-haired man said. "But don't think you've heard the last of this. Some of us are for calling a town meeting to decide our course of action. We shouldn't have to do your job for you."

"That's right, Fred," Bullock said gruffly. "You have no business trying to do my job. I wear the badge, I'll put an end to the gunfighting. If you meddle you'll only make matters worse." He angrily motioned with his right arm. "So for the last time, get the hell out of here."

Fred frowned and turned to go with the rest. "We won't forget your attitude, Marshal."

"I hope not," Bullock said, then grinned. "And Fred?"

"What?"

"Nice nightshirt. Tell Harriet she has good taste."

Some of the townsmen laughed.

Bullock faced Skye. "See the trouble I'm in because of Cord and you? I wish the two of you would settle this one way or the other so Beartown can go back to being a quiet little town where hardly anything ever happens."

"I'll be settling with Cord soon," Fargo vowed. "Speaking of which, I learned something today that will be of interest to you."

"Such as?"

Fargo told Bullock about his encounter with the cowhand in the hills west of the RC spread and related the news about how Cord had acquired the cattle to start the ranch.

"Stolen cattle?" Bullock repeated when Skye was done. "Damn! And some from the LT, no less. That's one of the biggest outfits in Texas. The man who owns it, Ira Beesom, is a crusty old coon from back in the Tennessee hills. He carved out his spread decades ago. Had to fight Indians and the Mexicans to do it."

"Beesom should be told."

The marshal jammed his six-shooter into his holster. "Unfortunately, you're right. And I'm the man who has to send word." His hefty shoulders sagged. "Beesom will likely want Cord's hide. It looks like my headaches are far from over."

Skye reclaimed the Sharps and made for the street. "Will you do me a favor and close up when you're through here. I need to get some shut-eye."

"You're not the only one," Bullock grumbled, then added as an afterthought. "Oh. There's something else we need to discuss."

Fargo stopped.

"I talked to the Cords about Tillman and Burt. They claimed they knew nothing about any attempt on your life. They maintain Tillman and Burt were acting on their own."

"And you believe them?"

"Hell, no. But I don't have proof the Cords gave the order, and without it there's nothing I can do. The same with these two here," Bullock said with a nod at the two men on the ground.

"I understand," Fargo said. "And if it's any comfort, I know you're trying your best. I don't envy you, Marshal. You're caught between a rock and a hard place."

"Ain't that the truth!" Bullock spat.

Skye walked out. Except for the doctor who was hurrying toward the livery, the street was again deserted. Only now lights were on all up and down Main Street. One of the buildings lit up was the Whitman residence. No sooner did he step foot on the boardwalk than one of the twins flung open the door and rushed out, a heavy blue robe wrapped tight around her green nightgown.

"Skye! Thank heaven you're all right!"

"Mercia?"

"Yes. Marcia is fixing a pot of coffee," Mercia said, taking him by the arm to lead him inside. She closed the door, then escorted him to the nearest chair. "Have a seat. You must be tired after your long day."

"I am," Fargo admitted, gratefully sinking down. "How was your day?"

"Forget about me. I want to hear about you. Gunshots woke us up a while ago. I saw Fred Reese going by the door and asked him what had happened. He told me a couple of men apparently tried to shoot you down at the livery but that you were okay." She perched on the edge of the desk. "He also said some nasty things about you. Fred and a good many other townspeople would like to see you sent packing."

"So I gathered."

"Care to tell me about it?"

Before Skye could respond, Marcia swept into the room. She was dressed identically to her sister. Offering a reserved smile as she approached, she said, "Coffee will be ready in a couple of minutes. Is there anything else I can get for you?"

"No," Fargo said, debating whether to confront her about her involvement with Lucas Cord. Strictly speaking, her personal affairs were none of his business. But he was intensely curious to learn why she had slept with him if she cared so much for Lucas, which she must if she had gone so far as to threaten June to stay away from Lucas or lose her life. It defied all common sense. There must be a logical explanation. But if he confronted her, she might deny the whole thing and demand he leave the house and forget about the job of finding her father, which would leave Mercia in the lurch. Perhaps, for the time being, his wisest move would be to say nothing about Lucas. The cattle, however, were another matter. "Not right now. I think I'll have some coffee and hit the sack." He paused. "Before I do, I should relay the good news. You won't have to worry about Lucas Cord bothering either of you much longer."

"Oh?" Mercia replied.

Marcia's lips compressed and she hugged her robe tighter to her. "Why is that."

"Because in a couple of weeks some men from Texas will show up in Beartown looking for the Cords, and if these gentlemen find Rory and Lucas they'll both have their necks stretched."

"But why?" Mercia asked.

"I found out today the Cords started their herd with cattle they stole down in Texas," Fargo disclosed. He noticed Marcia's features pale. "The marshal is contacting an important cattleman down there who won't take kindly to having had some of his stock rustled."

"Wonderful!" Mercia cried, clapping her hands in delight. "I can't wait to be rid of that foul Lucas Cord once and for all!"

Marcia, Fargo noticed, was not speaking. He remembered the incident that involved him in the whole mess, when Lucas grabbed Mercia's arm in the street, and wondered why Lucas had done so when by then he and Marcia were already heavily involved and had been for some time. That, too, made no sense.

"This is a great news story!" Mercia was saying. "I think it rates the first special edition in the short history of *The Beartown Chronicle*. By tomorrow afternoon we can have the papers out on the street, and by the day after tomorrow everyone in Beartown will know what rotten bastards the Cords are."

"We shouldn't do anything hasty," Marcia said.

Mercia glanced at her as if she couldn't believe her ears. "What's gotten into you? This is the biggest news story we've ever come across. Why, if Dad were here he'd be whooping for joy."

"Have you forgotten all the pointers he gave us about how to run a newspaper properly? Always check sources, remember? Always have stories verified before printing allegations. Never write a bad piece about someone simply because you don't like them."

"We're talking about the *Cords*, remember?" Mercia countered. "The same Cords who had this whole town quaking in its boots until Skye arrived. The same Cords we believe are responsible for our father's disappearance—and possibly his death. The same damn Cords—one of whom has bothered us more times than I care to recall."

"Maybe so," Marcia stood by her guns. "But I think we'll be making a grievous error if we print a story that makes wild, unsubstantiated accusations. No one has yet proven the Cords stole those cattle." She shot an accusing glance at Skye. "Where did you hear this tale, anyway?"

"From one of Cord's men, right before Lucas Cord killed him."

Mercia grinned like a cat that had just eaten a canary. "There!" she gloated. "What more proof do we need?"

"It's still not enough," Marcia insisted.

"How can you say that?"

"Hearsay isn't evidence. It's not proof that will hold up in court and has no business being reported as such in a newspaper."

Fargo had to interrupt. "I saw the evidence with my own eyes. And once those Texans get here, they'll be able to identify which cattle were theirs."

"I'm convinced," Mercia stated.

"Well, I'm not," Marcia said. "I refuse to have any part in printing baseless accusations."

"Fine," Mercia retorted. "I'll put out the special edition by myself. It doesn't have to be more than one page. I can handle all the work without you."

"You go right ahead," Marcia said, angrily spinning on her heels and stomping up the stairs. She went around the corner and a second later a door slammed so hard it seemed as if the entire house shook.

Mercia was stunned. She moved to the chair behind the desk and sat down. "I don't understand her at all anymore, and we used to be so close. How can she stand up for the Cords, of all people?"

"She must have a reason," Fargo said, and left it at that. Inwardly, he was thinking about all the harsh comments Marcia had made about the Cords prior to that night and about how Marcia had seemed genuinely pleased to have him looking into the disappearance of their father. That must have all been a sham, playacting on her part to deceive everyone else. But why did Marcia and Lucas want their relationship kept a secret? What else were they hiding?"

"Do you think I'm right?" Mercia inquired.

Fargo looked at her. "You're the newspaperwoman. If you think the story deserves a special edition, then go with your instincts."

Mercia glanced at the handpress. "If I identify the accusations as just that, legally and ethically I'll be in the clear but I'll still get the story out." She smacked her palm on the desktop. "By George, that's just what I'll do!" Rising, she started toward the stairs, then halted. "Do you mind pouring your own coffee? I need to talk with the marshal before I write my feature."

"I'll manage," Fargo said, and added, "You'll find

Bullock down at the livery with the doctor and the undertaker."

Mercia went up the stairs in a rush.

Fatigue crept along Fargo's limbs and shrouded his mind as he stood and walked down the hallway to his room. He leaned the Sharps on the wall, stretched, then reclined on his back and pulled his hat brim over his eyes. Upstairs, loud voices rose in a heated argument. The twins were still at each other's throats. What would Marcia do now? he pondered. Ride out to warn Lucas that the marshal knew about the rustled stock? The thought made him lift his hat and start to rise. If she rode off he wanted to trail her. Then he realized she wouldn't be going anywhere for quite a while. Bullock and the others were at the livery. Mercia would also be there soon. It was unlikely Marcia would try to head for the RC when she'd be seen leaving and her departure at such a late hour would make the marshal and Mercia very curious, if not downright suspicious. No, Marcia would wait until later when she could slip off unnoticed.

He sank down again. If he could manage a few hours sleep he would be as good as new in the morning. When Marcia headed for the RC, as he was sure she eventually would, he'd be her second shadow. He listened to the argument continue to rage upstairs. The girls were so loud some of the neighbors were bound to hear. Yet another benefit of living in a town or city; there was never any privacy. Their voices droned on and on, lulling him into the twilight realm of the sandman.

Marcia Whitman departed Beartown shortly before noon, and she did so in a clever fashion. Skye had kept an eye on her all morning without being obvious about it. During breakfast she had said little. Nor, for that matter, had Mercia. For the first time in their lives the twins were at odds with one another, not even speaking unless they had to. A chill gripped the house.

After breakfast Mercia hurried off to talk again with Marshal Bullock and the doctor. Marcia went upstairs. Skye waited in his room with the door open a crack so he would hear if she left. Soon she did, out the front. He went out the back. Moving along the rear of the buildings lining Main Street, he was able to keep track of her as she strolled down toward the livery. If she intended to leave then her plan was frustrated by the presence of June in the livery. Back to the house Marcia went, where she stayed until fifteen minutes before noon. Mercia had just gone to have her midday meal at Ruth's after working all morning in the office when Marcia came downstairs and ventured outside.

Once more Skye was ready. He heard the front door close and hastened out the back. Marcia made toward the west end of the town and paused across the street from the livery. Skye had to smile at her cleverness. During the noon hour few people stopped by the stable and June went off to have a bite to eat. The livery was deserted. Marcia quickly crossed, saddled her mare, and headed out of town, keeping the horse to a walk so as not to draw attention. Once beyond the town limits she turned due north and broke into a gallop.

Fargo ran to the livery, threw a saddle on the stallion, shoved the Sharps in the scabbard, and was in pursuit in minutes. Since he knew her destination he angled cross-country, well out of sight of the road Marcia was taking to the ranch, relying on the stallion's speed and endurance to get him well in front of her. Shortly thereafter he cut closer to the dirt road and reined up in the shelter of a cluster of pines. He didn't have long to wait.

Marcia Whitman had slowed to a canter when she went past, her hair glistening in the sunlight, her gaze fixed straight ahead. She never saw Skye.

He let her go several hundred yards before he moved from cover and paralleled her course. When she entered the hills he rode up into them, staying below the skyline while always keeping her in sight. She reached the boundary of the ranch, then did a strange thing. Stopping, she stood in the stirrups and waved her arm overhead again and again.

Now what was this? Fargo wondered, gazing at the distant buildings. They were too far off for anyone to be able to see her. To his surprise, within a minute a rider appeared, speeding in her direction. He was mystified until he remembered the man with the telescope the other day. The Cords must have someone constantly watching the approaches to their spread.

As the rider drew closer Fargo recognized the man:

Lucas Cord. Marcia rode out to meet him, and when they halted they quickly climbed down and embraced. Cord kissed her. She responded passionately, clinging to him as her hands stroked his face and neck. Then she began talking.

Skye could just barely make out their features, and almost immediately it became apparent that Cord did not like whatever Marcia was saying. Lucas gestured angrily, his voice rising although the words were not quite distinct enough to be understood from Skye's perch on the last hill. Marcia held her own, practically shouting as she jabbed a finger at Cord's chest. They argued for several minutes. At last Cord said something that prompted Marcia to leap into his arms and give him a kiss to end all kisses.

What was that all about? Fargo wondered. He wished he was closer so he could eavesdrop. Now he knew June had told the truth and Marcia was deeply involved with Lucas. But he was no nearer to learning the fate of Adam Whitman. He began to doubt the Cords had anything to do with the disappearance since it was unlikely Marcia would still be romantically linked with Lucas if the younger Cord had harmed her father.

The pair were huddled together, apparently making plans. Several times Lucas motioned at the ranch house. Marcia pointed toward town once. After a while they both nodded, then kissed again. Marcia stepped to her mare and Lucas helped her to mount.

Fargo knew she was heading back. He eased from the rim, dashed to the pinto, and went down the slope. All during the long ride into Beartown he pondered his next move. He should confront Marcia and force her to tell him everything she knew, but did he have the right? Her relationship with Lucas Cord was her business, a strictly personal matter into which he had no business prying. Maybe he should tell Mercia and let *her* pry. Marcia might resent it less.

He rode east of the road, as before, repeatedly glancing over his shoulder in case Marcia should come galloping along before he had a comfortable lead. Usually he kept to whatever cover was handy. But a mile from the hills he had to cross a stretch of nothing but grass and some sagebrush. For all of forty or fifty seconds he was in the open.

It was then the Ovaro jerked its head up and stared at the road. Fargo did the same, cursing at the sight of two RC cowhands on their way to the ranch from town. They spied him an instant later, and with loud whoops they drew their pistols and charged.

12

Skye Fargo reined to the left, touched his spurs to the stallion, and raced due east, drawing the pair away from the road. He used the sparse vegetation to the best advantage he could, weaving all the time to make himself a difficult target. The cowhands would soon be in pistol range. He had to stay far enough ahead so they wouldn't fire until the road was quite a ways back and Marcia wouldn't hear the gunshot.

The Ovaro seemed glad for another chance to ride like the wind. Accustomed to the wild, open spaces, the pinto became restless when confined in a stall for any length of time.

They skirted mesquite, took a shallow gully in a single jump, and swung to the northeast where ravines and canyons crisscrossed the land. Fargo hoped to avoid more bloodshed but the two cowhands had other ideas. Three-quarters of a mile from the road, one of the men snapped off a shot.

The slug came nowhere close. Fargo bent low and concentrated on reaching a canyon another mile farther. He saved his ammunition for when it would really be needed. The sun beat down on his back. The wind whipped his hair and threatened to strip away his hat at any second. Gradually the Ovaro gained ground on the RC men. Not much, but enough to discourage them from firing again.

Skye reached the mouth of the canyon safely. He saw what appeared to be a low earthen bank connecting the canyon walls and went over it without slackening his pace, which turned out to be a grave mistake. Too late he discovered the bank was actually the lip of a steep talus slope where once a section of canyon wall had stood. Loose rocks and dirt covered the slope from top to bottom. He was unable to stop as the pinto plunged headlong toward a bowl-shaped area below. Stones and dust spewed from under the big steed's scrambling hoofs. Despite a valiant try, the Ovaro lost its footing halfway to the bottom and fell.

Fargo felt the pinto's legs give and hurled himself from the saddle as the horse began to go down. The swirling dust prevented him from seeing the slope clearly. Consequently, he hit on his side instead of his shoulder. Pain lanced through his chest. In a heartbeat he was tumbling end over end, jagged stones gouging into him each time he struck the ground.

He collided with a large, hard object, probably a boulder, and his senses swam. The next thing he knew he was lying on his stomach in the midst of a dust cloud and listening to the Ovaro whinny nearby. His head throbbed. He struggled to stand but the dizziness became worse. With a supreme effort he managed to get to his knees.

Those cowhands would be there at any moment! Skye reached for his Colt, his fingers closing on empty air. The gun was gone, dislodged during his tumble, lying somewhere above him on the talus slope. Of all the luck! He heaved upright, staggered, and started to scour the ground. The dust was like a veil. He couldn't see more than a yard in any direction, and the Ovaro was nowhere around.

He took a few strides higher, leaning over so he could see the ground better. The dust stung his eyes, making them water, compelling him to blink to clear them. Scrambling upward, he dislodged more rocks and dirt, contributing to the cloud. He halted in frustration and impatiently waited for the dust to settle enough to permit him to see the slope. Oddly enough, there had been no sound of hoofbeats above. Perhaps the hands suspected a trap and had stopped a few hundred yards from the canyon. If so, it would give him the time he needed to find the damn Colt.

The dust began to clear. He spied the Ovaro thirty feet from the base of the slope, covered with dirt and scratches but apparently not seriously hurt. The stock of the Sharps jutted from the scabbard, tempting him to fetch it rather than continue hunting for the revolver. He turned to make another sweep, his head feeling fine at last, and froze on hearing a mocking laugh.

"Lookin' for this, mister?" asked a burly man standing a dozen yards below the rim. In his right hand was a leveled pistol. In his left hand was Skye's Colt.

"I reckon he is, Bill," said a man on horseback at the top, a rifle tucked against his shoulder.

Fargo held his arms out from his sides, confirming he was unarmed. "I don't suppose you gents would be willing to let me collect my pinto and gun and ride back to Beartown?"

The man on the horse snickered. "Not on your life, Trailsman. You've killed several friends of ours. We figure we owe you."

"You watch this hombre, Aaron, while I get his critter yonder," said Bill, who gave himself plenty of room as he went around Skye, both revolvers aimed at Skye's stomach.

The man on the horse, Aaron, wagged the rifle barrel. "Come on up here, mister. No fancy tricks or I'm liable to blow your head clean off."

Having no other choice, Fargo walked to the rim. He saw the one named Bill trying to catch hold of the Ovaro, but every time the man reached for the dangling reins the stallion would move a few yards.

"If your horse keeps that up, Bill is likely to get good and riled and shoot it," Aaron commented.

Fargo was about to call to the stallion when the other cowhand made a frantic lunge and seized the reins. Muttering oaths, the man wheeled and led the Ovaro toward them.

"Must be your lucky day," Aaron said with a smirk.

"I'm surprised you boys are still in this part of the country," Fargo responded. "I know I wouldn't want to be in your boots and still be here when those Texans show up."

"What Texans?" Aaron asked, straightening.

"Didn't you hear? The marshal found out about the rustling Cord did in Texas. He's sent word to the LT outfit. Hope you don't mind having your neck stretched."

Aaron's face became a mask of worry. "You're lyin', mister," he replied angrily. "The marshal did no such thing."

"Do you really think Bullock wouldn't do a thing once he learned the truth about how Cord started his ranch with a stolen herd? A week or two from now those Texans will ride into Beartown looking for blood." He paused for effect. "You know how Texans can be when they're mad."

Aaron frowned and chewed on his lip. "Where did you learn about the Texas business?" he demanded.

"One of the ranch hands told me."

"Now I know you're lying. None of us would turn in Rory Cord. What is this hand's name?"

"He never told me," Fargo said. "He was shot by Lucas Cord before I could find out."

The news made Aaron do a double take and lower the rifle an inch. "Lucas would never kill any of us," he said, his voice lacking true conviction.

"Lucas isn't Rory," Fargo countered. "I'm willing to bet one of your men has turned up missing. Never came back to the ranch last night and hasn't been heard from since yesterday morning."

"Hinds is his name," Aaron said. "Rory sent us into Beartown to look for him but he wasn't there and no one had seen him around." He lowered the rifle another inch. "Damn! You must be telling the truth."

Neither of them spoke until Bill came up the steep slope with the stallion. Aaron related the information Skye had just imparted and both cowhands glared at him.

"You'd be smart to let me go," Fargo urged.

"Even if you're right about Hinds, we still have a score to settle with you," Bill snapped. "We'll deal with Lucas Cord later. Or Rory will. Right now we're taking you to the ranch so the boss can finish what he started at the restaurant."

Fargo took a step toward the pinto, his eyes on the Sharps. If he could get behind his horse, he might be able to slip the rifle from the scabbard without being noticed.

"Hold on!" Bill declared. He turned and reached over the Ovaro to pull the Sharps out. "I wouldn't want you trying something stupid."

"Keep your hands where I can see them all the time," Aaron added. "Unless you want to save Rory the trouble of hanging you. We wouldn't mind leaving your carcass here for the buzzards and the coyotes."

"I'll behave," Fargo lied, and mounted. He had to wait while Bill ran to a dun gelding, then all three of them headed toward the green hills with Aaron in front and Bill to his rear.

"Where were you coming from when we saw you?" Bill asked.

"Canada."

"You have a smart mouth, mister. I'll be glad to see it turn all blue and your tongue poke out when that noose tightens around your neck."

Skye yearned for a distraction. Neither man was close enough for him to jump without being shot. They were being cagey, taking no chances at all. Unless they made a mistake, in another hour or two he would be swinging from a tree on the RC spread. Neither had thought to search him so he still had the Arkansas toothpick, but a fat lot of good it would do against two men bound to be quick on the trigger.

As the hills grew nearer, Skye was constantly on the lookout for a way to escape. Under no circumstances could he allow them to take him to the ranch. Once there his fate would be sealed as Rory Cord was certain to keep him under heavy guard until the moment he danced from the end of a rope. But no opportunities presented themselves.

He spied the ribbon of road off on the left and saw that Aaron was slanting toward the point where the road entered the hills. As his gaze roved to the right his hopes rose a bit. A wide dry wash twelve feet deep bisected the pair of hills closest to the road, and he figured they would pass within forty yards of it. Not much of an escape route but it would have to do.

Aaron had been glancing over his shoulder a lot when they first started out, but now he rode staring straight ahead, apparently convinced Skye would not give them any trouble.

Fargo casually twisted his neck to see Bill out of the corner of his eye. The burly man had pulled a small leather pouch from his shirt pocket and was in the process of rolling a cigarette. Bill had Skye's Colt wedged under his belt, the Sharps resting across his thighs.

He changed his mind. Instead of trying for the dry wash and risking a slug between the shoulder blades, he would try the direct approach. Since neither of these men was disposed to show him any mercy, he wasn't about to show them any. They had started this; he would finish it.

For the next minute Fargo rode with his shoulders slumped, his chin bowed, as if dejected, too upset by his capture to care about anything else. He noticed Aaron look at him and smirk. Gripping the reins firmly, he tensed, waited until Aaron swung forward, then abruptly wheeled the Ovaro in a sharp turn and rode straight at Bill. The burly man had no chance to do more than glance up and gape, his cigarette makings in his right hand, his revolver and his reins held loosely in his left.

Fargo had the pinto alongside the dun in a second. His right fist smashed into Bill's mouth as the man tried to bring his gun to bear. Bill rocked backward, arms outflung, and Fargo lunged, grabbing his Colt and wrenching it free. Shifting in a twinkling, he swept his right arm around and up, aiming at Aaron's head as the cowhand was in the act of turning his horse sideways for a better shot. The Colt banged twice. Aaron catapulted from the saddle and crashed into some sagebrush.

Shifting again, Fargo slammed the barrel of his gun onto Bill's forehead just as Bill raised his own gun. The burly cowhand flew off the far side of the dun and landed on his back. Game to the last, Bill promptly pushed onto one elbow, his revolver rising. Fargo fired two more shots. Crimson dots blossomed between Bill's eyes and he stiffened, then went limp.

Skye glanced at Aaron, making sure he was dead. He reloaded, spotted the Sharps lying in the grass, and climbed down to retrieve it. By now Marcia was probably halfway to Beartown so he doubted she had heard the gunfire. She might become suspicious of where he had been when he rode into town after her, but it couldn't be helped. Aaron and Bill had ruined his plan to get there before her.

He mounted and rode south. Bullock would need to be told about the bodies, and then he would have a long talk with Mercia and find out how much she knew about Marcia and Lucas Cord. Eager to get back, he angled to the road so he could make better time. The rest of the ride was spent reviewing everything that had happened.

Beartown bustled with typical afternoon activity when Skye turned down Main Street to the livery. June was out front, watering a horse at the trough. She smiled at the sight of him until she noticed the cuts and dust on the Ovaro and his own dust-caked frame. Concern lining her features, she moved to the doorway.

"Good Lord! Are you all right?"

Skye stopped and stepped down. "A little worse for wear, but otherwise I'm fine."

"Have you been playing in the dirt?"

He chuckled. "Not quite. Two of the Cord bunch saw fit to give me a hard time."

"Are they—?" June asked, leaving the sentence unfinished.

"As dead as they come," Fargo confirmed, leading the pinto to the trough. He touched one of the many small cuts on its flank and the skin quivered. The worst of the wounds was a three-inch gash on the right thigh.

"Your poor horse," June said. "Want me to give it a good rubdown and wash all that dirt out of those cuts? There's also some salve inside that my brother swears by. Fights infection and helps wounds heal."

"I don't want to put you to any bother."

June smiled coyly. "What are friends for?" She came next to him and spoke softly. "How about supper again tonight? If not, then how about just stopping by when you have the chance? It doesn't matter how late."

"I can't make any promises," Fargo said. "Something tells me things may come to a head with the Cords soon. I'll have to pass on supper, but if I can I'll pay you a visit sometime after eight."

"I can't wait," June responded, her frank sensual gaze hinting at tantalizing rewards if he did show up.

Fargo peered into the livery, seeking Marcia's mare. "How long ago did Marcia Whitman ride in?"

"Marcia?" June repeated in the same tone she might use to mention a rattlesnake. "Haven't seen her all day. Her horse was gone when I came back about one o'clock but she hasn't brought it back yet."

Where could she be? Fargo wondered. Touching the brim of his hat, he headed for the Whitman house, the

124

Sharps under his left arm. Marcia should have arrived within the past half hour. Perhaps she hadn't gone directly to the livery because June was there. Acting on a hunch, he went across the street and along an alley until he could see the rear of the Whitman place. There was the mare by the back door.

He retraced his steps to the street and sauntered to the restaurant. Few townsfolk were eating so early. In a back corner sat Ruth and one of the twins, each sipping coffee. At his approach the twin grinned.

"Good news! I'll have the special edition done in about an hour. I'd hoped to finish it sooner, but it's harder than I thought doing all the work myself."

Fargo sat down across from her and checked her earlobes. Both were the same size. "Marcia still won't help?"

"Are you kidding? She's been gone most of the day. Probably out for one of her rides. Whenever she's mad she stays away longer than usual," Mercia said.

"Care for a bite to eat?" Ruth asked him.

"Don't mind if I do. And some coffee would be nice," Fargo said. He waited until she was in the kitchen before looking at Mercia. "Has it ever occurred to you that Marcia might have a particular place to go when she rides off by herself?"

"Where, for instance?" Mercia rejoined, and took another sip.

"The Cord spread."

"Are you out of your mind? Why would she want to go there?"

"To see Lucas Cord."

Mercia's expression betrayed her perplexity. "She hates Lucas as much as I do. There's no reason in the world for her to see him."

"What if I was to tell you Marcia is head over heels in love with Lucas?"

"I'd say you've been out in the sun too long and it's scrambled your brain."

"Brace yourself," Fargo said, and detailed the meeting he had witnessed plus the information he had learned about Marcia threatening a former sweetheart of Cord's, although he felt it best not to mention June by name.

Mercia listened in amazement that gradually transformed into fiery anger. When he concluded, she slammed her cup down on the table, splashing coffee on her dress and her arms, then rose with her fists balled. "All this time she's been playing us for fools! How could she like Lucas after all that vermin has done?"

"People do strange things when they're in love," was all Fargo could think of to say.

"She owes me an explanation," Mercia declared, spinning. "You stay here. This is a personal matter to be settled between the two of us. I'll be back when it's all over."

Fargo watched her storm out and settled back in his chair. After Ruth brought his meal he took his time eating and polished off five cups of piping hot coffee. Twilight came. Then night in all its starry glory shrouded Beartown when Skye finally set the cup aside and gazed out the front window.

Ruth stopped at the table. "Didn't you say Mercia was coming back?"

"So she said."

"Hmmmm. Seems to me she should have been here by now."

The same thought had occurred to Skye, although he'd told himself the twins might go on arguing until dawn if their past behavior was any indication. He paid the bill, walked to the boardwalk, and noticed the windows in the Whitman house were dark, the door partially open. Odd, he reflected, that neither of the sisters had bothered to light a lantern yet.

He crossed to the door and listened. Inside all was deathly still. Easing the door open with his foot, he slipped into the office to discover the floor was coated with sheets of paper, most torn in half, some shredded into tiny pieces. He picked up a few sections. The print was difficult to read, but the single large headline, CORDS ACCUSED OF BEING RUSTLERS, told him the special edition wouldn't be hitting the streets any time soon.

"Mercia?" Skye called, and when no answer was forthcoming he stepped to the base of the stairs. "Mercia? Marcia? Is anyone home?"

Silence reigned.

He took the stairs two at a stride, pausing when he reached the second floor. "Mercia? Where are you?" On the right were two doors, on the left, one. Each turned out to be a bedroom. The one on the left, judging by the clothes hanging in a closet and a pair of large boots at the foot of the bed, had been Adam Whitman's. He was surprised to find the twins had separate rooms. Possibly because they were identical and did most everything together, he had assumed they would share one. In the last bedroom he found clothes scattered over the bed and the carpet. Drawers had been pulled out, the contents upended.

Puzzled, Skye walked to the top of the stairs. Where could the twins have gone? He decided to see if the mare was still out back and hurried down, but as he turned toward the hallway a low groan filled the newspaper office. Instantly he palmed the Colt and whirled.

Again someone moaned, from the vicinity of the big desk.

Avoiding the scattered newspapers, he glided cautiously forward until he spied a pair of legs jutting from behind the desk. In three bounds he was beside it, staring down in horror at Mercia Whitman. She lay flat on her back, a wide stain covering the front of her dress, a knife embedded in her chest.

13

Skye Fargo dashed to the front door, intent on going for the doctor, when a loud thump from the rear of the house made him pivot and crouch. The back door was wide open. Figuring Marcia must be about to ride off, he sprinted down the hall. He was halfway along when a rifle barrel was thrust inside. His reaction was immediate and swift. With extended arms he dived, hitting the floor as the rifle boomed. Then he rolled to the right and snapped off an answering shot that shattered the doorjamb just as the rifle disappeared.

Footsteps sounded, then the thud of hoofs.

Skye was erect and to the door in a flash, but already Marcia and the mare were no more than vague shapes in the night. He lifted the Colt, about to fire, dominated by his anger over Mercia. Just in time he realized he was on the verge of shooting a woman in the back. Reluctantly, he lowered the Colt. There would be another day. Marcia and Lucas hadn't seen the last of him, not by a long shot.

He ran to the front of the house, emerging as Marshal Bullock and several townsmen converged.

"What's all the shooting?" the lawman demanded.

"Marcia just tried to kill me," Fargo answered, continuing before anyone else could comment. "You need to fetch the doc. Mercia has been stabbed. Her sister did it."

Bullock was all business as he ordered a skinny man to run for the doctor, then directed the others to stay outside while he followed Fargo in. "Where is she?"

Skye lit a lantern and deposited it on the desk. "Right here."

The marshal glowered when he saw her. His thick lips clamped together. He looked like a mad old bull ready to gore anything that moved. "I thought these girls were two peas in a pod. Why would Marcia stab the one person she was closest to, the only kin she has left? What do you know about it?"

"Marcia has been seeing Lucas Cord on the sly. I told Mercia at the restaurant and she came over here to question her sister."

Bullock glanced at the Trailsman. "Seeing Lucas Cord? Well, I'll be damned!"

"Marcia just left. I'm going after her," Fargo said, moving to the doorway.

"You'll wait for me," the lawman said. "Since this crime was committed in my jurisdiction, I have the legal right to track down the culprit no matter where she goes. After we get Mercia to the doctor's, the two of us will finish this dirty business once and for all."

Although Fargo preferred to ride alone, in this instance he decided not to make an issue of it. Marcia was undoubtedly on her way to the RC ranch. If he went alone, the Cords and the rest of the rustlers would shoot him on sight. With the marshal along, the Cords might think twice before opening fire. Killing a lawman would bring the federal marshal and possibly the army down on their heads and the Cords certainly wouldn't want that.

The doctor arrived, made a cursory examination, and asked for help in getting Mercia to his office. Someone brought a wide plank. Fargo assisted four townsmen in gently placing her on it and carefully carrying her to the doctor's. By then a large crowd had gathered and followed all the way down the street.

Fargo stood just inside the office, watching the doctor prepare his instruments. "What do you think, Doc?" he asked.

"I honestly can't say. She's lost considerable blood, but I have no way of telling if the blade has punctured a lung or severed a major artery. She could be bleeding internally. I don't believe it touched her heart or she would already be dead."

Bullock moved to the door. "Do your best. I might be gone for quite a while, but I'll stop by first thing after I get back to town."

Skye trailed the marshal outside where it seemed as if the entire population of Beartown was waiting. Some shouted at Bullock, demanding to know what had happened.

"Mercia Whitman has been stabbed. The doc is working on her now and I don't want anyone to bother him. So clear out!"

"Who stabbed her?" a middle-aged woman asked, glancing spitefully at Skye.

"It looks like her sister did it. I'll know more once I've caught her," Bullock answered. "Now, for the second and final time, I want all of you to go about your business."

Many grumbled, but they broke up, some pointing at Skye and whispering.

"This town is a powder keg," Bullock said softly. "If I don't put an end to the killing, I'm afraid I'll have a pack of vigilantes on my hands. And we both know where that can lead."

Fargo nodded. Decent citizens, when aroused, often became more bloodthirsty than the outlaws they rose up against. Sometimes innocent people were shot or hung for the flimsiest of reasons. Vigilantes seldom bothered with proving a person's guilt. And if a vigilante band formed in Beartown, he was sure to be one of the first ones they went after because quite a few townsmen blamed him for causing all the trouble.

No one was at the livery when they got there, and it took only a few minutes to saddle their mounts. The marshal's horse was a huge black stallion, even bigger than the Ovaro, able to bear his great weight without difficulty.

Neither of them spoke until they were well on the road toward the ranch. It was Bullock who glanced at Skye and said, "Tell me again about your being shot at after you found Mercia."

Puzzled, Fargo did so.

"Then you didn't actually see Marcia Whitman do the shooting?" the marshal asked. "All you saw was someone riding off into the night and you figured it must be her."

Fargo thought for a moment, recalling the figure that had raced away from the house. In the dark it had been impossible to see much more than a black silhouette. "True," he said.

"Damn," Bullock muttered. "I'd have a hard time proving a case against her in court on just your say-so."

"You don't think *I* stabbed Mercia and lied about Marcia doing it?"

"Hell no. You're not the kind to go around killing women. It takes a yellowbelly or a weakling to do something like that. Besides, I happened to walk past the Whitman place about fifteen minutes before the shots rang out and I heard the twins arguing inside. They were practically screaming at each other." Bullock paused. "But since you didn't get a clear look at Marcia, and since no one actually saw her stab Mercia, I've got my work cut out for me in proving she did it."

By the time they reached the hills the wind had picked up, rustling the grass and the sagebrush. Clouds in ever increasing numbers obscured the shining stars and the temperature dropped a few degrees.

"Just what we need," Bullock commented. "We're in for a storm."

Fargo pulled his hat down so the wind wouldn't blow it off. A few scattered raindrops fell. Over the next couple of miles the drops fell more frequently. The sky became completely overcast, shrouding the landscape in total darkness. When they rode out of the hills onto the RC ranch the wind increased even more, shrieking as it buffeted them and their mounts.

He spied lights glowing in the distance, pinpoints of brightness in a sea of ink. His right hand strayed to the Colt and rested on the butt. "They might be waiting for someone to show up," he remarked.

"I reckon," Bullock said. "If she's told them what she did." He glanced at Skye. "I've never had to arrest a woman before. It sort of makes me feel uncomfortable. Must be because my folks raised me to regard all women as ladies. Goes against the grain."

"I felt that way once," Fargo said. "Years ago, before I ran across some women who were every bit as dangerous as any man. Killers come in all shapes, sizes, and sexes."

They approached the buildings in silence. Not that they need have worried about being heard. The wind howled like a chorus of wolves, drowning out all sound, and the rain descended in a steady but light drizzle.

"You let me go in by myself," Bullock said. "Cord won't shoot if he doesn't see you."

"All right," Fargo agreed, "but at the first sign of trouble I'll be there."

The marshal smiled, his teeth white in the night. "I'm counting on it."

No one was outside. The barn and the bunkhouse were both dark. Lanterns blazed inside the ranch house, though, and shadows flitted across the curtains now and again. Four horses were in the corral, none wearing saddles.

Fargo hung back, drawing the Colt as Bullock rode up to within fifteen feet of the front door. A shadow attached itself to one of the curtains, then disappeared. Before Bullock could speak, the front door opened and out strode Rory Cord, a shotgun in his hands.

"Is that you, Marshal?"

"It's me, Rory."

"Kind of late for a social call, isn't it?" Cord asked, peering past the lawman in an effort to see if anyone else was out there.

Fargo stayed still, positive the rustler wouldn't spot him, so perfectly did he blend into the backdrop of the night. He saw someone else emerge and recognized Rebecca Cord.

"This ain't no social visit," Bullock was saying. "I'm hunting for Marcia Whitman."

Rory snorted. "What would she be doing here? Those girls hate me. They think I had something to do with their pa vanishing, but I didn't."

"Is Lucas home?"

"What's my son have to do with anything?"

"Lucas and Marcia Whitman have been seeing each other for quite some time. Or didn't you know?"

Rebecca whispered to Rory. He shook his head and motioned for her to go inside, but she stayed put. "You must be drunk, Marshal," Rory said. "My son would never take up with one of those uppity twins." He hefted the shotgun. "Now why don't you ride on back to town? I heard about you sending word to some fellers in Texas, claiming I stole some of their cattle. If you weren't a lawman, I'd blast you right out of that saddle."

"I want to check your house and the other buildings," Bullock said.

Fargo saw Cord train the shotgun on the marshal's chest and thought he heard the click of a hammer being pulled back.

"I can't allow that, Fred. Leave before you make me do something I'll regret."

Bullock shook his head. "I have a job to do," he said, and went to climb down.

"Stop!" Cord cried, taking a step. "Damn it all, Fred, I don't want to shoot a lawman. Use your head and get the hell out of here, pronto."

The marshal started to lift his left foot out of the stirrup. "Sorry, Rory."

"So am I," Cord said.

The booming of the shotgun was like thunder to Fargo's ears. He spurred the Ovaro forward as Bullock twisted sharply and fell. Cord looked up, saw him coming, and reached into a shirt pocket for another shotgun shell, backpedaling as he did. Fargo aimed at Cord's chest and fired, but at the very instant the Colt bucked he saw Cord lift the shotgun higher. The slug smashed into the stock, tearing the shotgun from Cord's fingers. Fargo went to shoot again when the whipping wind blew a drop of rain into his right eye, momentarily blurring his vision. He hesitated, giving Cord time to dash inside on Rebecca's heels and slam the door behind him.

Fargo drew rein and jumped down beside the marshal, covering him. Bullock had sat up, his fleshy left hand pressed over his right shoulder, a grimace on his face.

"The son of a bitch shot me! I didn't think he'd do it."

"We've got to move!" Fargo advised. No sooner were the words out of his mouth than one of the windows shattered and a rifle poked its wicked muzzle out. He snapped off two shots, hoping it wasn't Rebecca holding the gun, and the rifle was withdrawn.

"Give me a hand," Bullock said.

Fargo grabbed the marshal under the left shoulder and heaved. It was like trying to lift a ten-ton boulder. Bullock came off the ground slowly, grunting and wheezing, and swayed when he straightened. "Can you reach the barn?" Fargo asked.

"If I have to crawl."

Wailing like a horde of banshees the storm broke in earnest as Skye grabbed the Ovaro's reins and brought up the rear, his eyes roving from one window to another. Strangely, Cord didn't fire again. Once he was in the barn, sheltered from the driving rain, he stood by the door while Marshal Bullock sat down with his back to a stall. "You need doctoring," he said.

"It will have to wait. I'm not leaving without Rory Cord."

"You're in no shape to arrest him."

Bullock mustered a wan grin. "I could with your help."

"Cord will die before he'll let you take him in," Fargo pointed out while listening to the raindrops batter the sides and roof of the barn, effectively preventing him from hearing any sounds from outside short of a gunshot. If Cord were to try and sneak up on them, they wouldn't know it until too late. Suddenly the lanterns in the house were extinguished. He watched the front door but nothing happened.

"I can still use my pistol," Bullock said. "You go in after him and I'll cover you."

"He might be expecting us to try a stunt like that," Fargo said. "We'd be better off making him come to us."

"How?"

Skye kept his eyes on the house in case Cord should try something. He wondered where the remaining ranch hands were and if Lucas and Marcia were around. "Cord isn't a patient man," he said after a bit. "He'll want to take care of us quickly, and the best time is right now while the storm hides his movements. So if we sit tight he'll come looking for us."

"Makes sense," Bullock said.

"Can you hold out until then?" Fargo asked.

"I think so," the lawman answered. He had pulled back his vest and unbuttoned his shirt to examine the wound. "I caught some buckshot and it hurts like hell, but the bleeding has already stopped."

Fargo squatted and leaned against the partially open door. Occasionally a gust of wind and rain would strike him in the face and he would have to wipe his sleeve across his eyes.

"It surprises me that Cord is still here," Bullock said.

"He knows I've sent word to Texas. If I was him I'd be pulling freight for other parts of the country."

"The Texans won't get here for a week or better. He has plenty of time to wrap things up here."

Bullock snapped his fingers. "I'll bet he might even try to sell off the ranch or just the stock and leave with enough pocket money to get him wherever he wants to go. So far only a few people know how he got his start."

The statement made Fargo think of the special edition of the *Chronicle* Marcia had destroyed. Was that her motive? To keep the news from spreading so the Cords would have time to hastily dispose of the cattle? Had Mercia caught her ripping up the newspapers and tried to stop her? Was that why Mercia had been stabbed?

"Mind if I speak my mind?" Bullock inquired.

"About what?"

"You. I'm glad you're here, Fargo. This sort of business is new to me. I was a constable back in Illinois for a few years, then drifted west when the town council let a few of us go. Worked at odd jobs to make ends meet. Then this position came along and I applied, never believing I'd be picked. But I was and I've tried to do the best I know how."

"I'd say you've done fine."

"Thanks. From a man like you that's a real compliment." The lawman sighed. "I'm glad you're here because I don't handle a gun very well and it's obvious you do. I've seen more dead men since you hit town than in all the years since I was born." He chuckled. "They should call you the Shootist, not the Trailsman."

Fargo grinned, then turned when a horse in the corral whinnied loudly. He slowly stood and took three strides. Was it his imagination or was there a commotion in the corral?

"What's the matter?" Bullock asked. He had his pistol out.

"I don't know yet," Fargo said. "Sit there while I go see." He hurried to the rear of the barn, able to distinguish the individual stalls and the animals occupying them. There should be a back door, he reasoned, and after running his hands over the wall for a minute his fingers came in contact with a vertical crack and felt cool air blowing through it. Seconds later he found a wooden latch.

Relying on the wind and the rain to muffle any noise, Skye worked the latch and pushed the door open an inch. Squinting so the rain wouldn't get into his eyes, he peered toward the corral and was shocked to see a black shape looming in the night not six feet away. The instant he laid eyes on the figure a shotgun blasted.

14

The storm saved Fargo's life.

Whoever fired the shotgun did so hastily, unleashing the buckshot from the hip instead of from the shoulder. Under ordinary circumstances, at such close range, it was doubtful anyone could miss. But the driving rain and wind, striking the figure full in the face, threw off the person's aim. So the buckshot ripped through the door several inches to the right of Fargo's shoulder, creating a hole the size of his fist, yet sparing the Trailsman.

By then Skye was in motion, diving to the ground to avoid a possible second shot. He rolled onto his back, his Colt trained on the door, unsure if he heard the dull thud of hoofs outside or whether it was the rain striking the barn.

"Fargo?" Marshal Bullock called. "Are you all right?"

Since to answer would give away his position, Skye said nothing. He warily rose to his knees and inched to the door, which was being buffeted by the wind and smacking repeatedly shut and open again. His head low, he dared a peek at the corral. Dimly, he saw two figures beside a pair of horses. He believed the animals had been saddled and guessed that the duo were preparing to ride off. Was it Rory and Rebecca? He lifted the Colt to fire, then checked himself. In the dark and the rain he couldn't tell which one was Rebecca, and after she had let him get away the other day after having the drop on him, he didn't want to shoot her.

Quickly, the pair mounted and galloped out of the corral. In seconds the storm swallowed them up.

"Fargo? Are you there?" Bullock shouted, sounding closer.

"I'm here, Fred," Skye responded, and rose. He saw

the lawman's enormous bulk moving toward him. "You shouldn't be on your feet."

"I thought you'd been shot," Bullock said. Stopping, he leaned against a stall and wheezed. "What the hell happened, anyway?"

"Two people just rode off. One tried to cut me in half with a shotgun."

"Cord and his wife?"

"I couldn't tell," Fargo said, moving to the marshal's side. "And it would be a waste of time for me to go after them. I couldn't find them in this storm and the rain will wash away their tracks as soon as they make them." He scratched his chin. "If it was the Cords, they picked the perfect time to leave."

"Let's check the house."

"I'll check it," Fargo said, putting a hand under the lawman's shoulder. "You'll rest until I get back, then we'll wait for the storm to end and get you to Beartown so the doc can have a look at you."

"I'm not crippled," Bullock groused.

"Someone has to watch our horses in case there are some of Cord's men around," Fargo said, even though he doubted there were any since they would have showed themselves earlier. He helped the lawman to the front of the barn, then moved to the entrance and scanned the ranch house and the bunkhouse.

Off in the distance lightning sparkled, followed seconds later by the rumble of thunder.

"Watch your back," Bullock said.

"Always," Fargo replied, and was off in a flash, weaving to make it harder for any concealed gunmen to bring him down. His boots smacked onto the rain-soaked ground, spraying mud over the bottom of his leggings. Rain struck his cheeks and mouth, but by tilting his hat brim he was able to shield his eyes. The ranch house front door was closed. Rather than bother with the latch, he gathered speed, lowered his right shoulder, and barreled into the door like a battering ram. Wood splintered, the lock gave way, and he plunged into deeper darkness, landing on his hands and knees on a bare wood floor.

He spied a chair to his left and promptly rolled behind it, then squatted, probing the interior for movement. All was quiet. A cool breeze on his left cheek caused him to glance toward the rear of the house where the back door hung wide open. Certain the Cords were gone, he nonetheless took no chances. On cat's feet he prowled around the house, inspecting every room, until he confirmed they had indeed left.

Next came the bunkhouse. The bunks were empty, there was a pile of dirty pans and dishes in a wooden bucket, and the coals in the potbellied stove were cold. No one had lived there for a day or more.

Skye went back to the house, lit a lantern, and looked in the cupboards for medical supplies. He found a bottle of tincture in a drawer in the bedroom and was returning to the living room when footsteps shuffled outside and the door was flung open. In the blink of an eye he streaked the Colt out and swiveled.

"Don't shoot!" Bullock said. "It's only me."

"You were supposed to wait in the barn," Fargo said, twirling the revolver into his holster.

"I saw the light come on and figured it was safe to come over," Bullock said. He moved to a sofa and sank into it with a pronounced sigh. "My shoulder is worse. You might have to pluck the buckshot out yourself if the storm doesn't break soon."

"I'm no doctor."

The marshal gingerly touched his wound. "If infection sets in I could lose this arm. Ever see a one-armed lawman?"

"Can't say as I have."

Bullock nodded. "I'd be washed up. My job means everything to me, Fargo, and I'd rather die than have to start over again at something else." He nodded at the stove. "Heat up some water, find a knife, and get to carving. I promise not to kick up a fuss."

Outside, a streak of lightning lit up a window and moments later thunder shook the building. The rain had intensified and was now a deluge.

Against Skye's better judgment, he nodded and walked to the stove. By all indications the storm would take hours to run its course. And he well knew how lead embedded deep in flesh soon brought on severe infections. Bullock was right. Something had to be done, the sooner the better. A stack of wood provided the means of producing a roaring blaze, and once the room was toasty he stepped to the kitchen area and rummaged through various drawers seeking a knife with a thin blade. He found a carving knife, a butcher knife, even a hunting knife, but none that would do the job properly. With no other recourse he drew the Arkansas toothpick and went back to the stove to heat it in the fire.

Bullock had removed his vest and shirt. Drying blood caked his shoulder and half of his chest. He eased onto his back and glanced at Skye. "Ever done this before?"

"A few times."

"Did your patients live?" Bullock asked with a grin.

Fargo pretended to think for a bit. "One did, as I recollect."

"You sure know how to inspire a man with confidence."

Once the tip of the toothpick was red hot, Fargo carried the knife and a clean towel to the sofa. The lawman stared at the toothpick and gulped. "Are you ready?"

"Whenever you are. And don't pay me no mind if I faint." Bullock raised his vest to his lips and clamped his teeth down on a corner of the leather.

It took over an hour. There were eight balls to dig out in all, and five were three inches deep. Fargo had to carefully insert the knife into each hole and probe until the blade touched the ball, then use the tip to work the ball loose and eventually pry it out. Bullock grunted repeatedly, his face flushed beet red, the veins on his thick neck standing out, his brow coated with beads of sweat. When at last Fargo set the blade aside and applied tincture to the wounds, the lawman was barely conscious. Skye dressed the shoulder as best he could, then settled down to wait for the storm to abate.

He sat in a chair and pondered his next move. Given all the Cords had put him through, he had no intention of letting them escape. He'd trail them to the ends of the earth if need be. But a little common sense told him he needn't go that far. Since both Lucas and Rory had women along, it was unlikely either would enter the desolate country to the south of Beartown. Nor were they likely to go north where hostile Indians waited to scalp unwary whites. They might go west along the Oregon Trail, but such travel was best done in the company of a large group for safety's sake. To his way of thinking, the Cords were probably traveling east. They could hide out in any one of dozens of towns dotting the plains.

East he would go come first light. He doubted Rory or Lucas would tempt fate by staying near the ranch or in Beartown. As news of their rustling activities spread, all hands would turn against them. They would be outcasts, sought by the law and the Texans bound to arrive sooner or later.

He heard Bullock snoring against the backdrop of the rain. Far to the north more thunder growled. The warmth from the stove seeped into his pores, making him drowsy. His eyes closed and he started to doze off. He resisted for a while, knowing it was foolish to fall asleep in the home of an enemy. But the Cords and their men were gone; he had nothing to worry about. That thought tempered his caution, and before he knew it he, too, was asleep.

His ears registered the loud crash seconds before his brain flared to life and he sat up with a start, blinking his eyes as he tried to focus and concentrate. He saw Bullock also trying to rouse himself, and then a blast of cold air and moisture flooded the room and he twisted to see a drenched Rory Cord standing just inside the open front door with a revolver clutched in his slick right hand.

"Not a move, either of you!"

Fargo tensed, his hands in his lap. If he tried for his Colt, Rory would put a slug into him before he could clear leather. His only hope was to stall and wait for an opening. "Hello Cord," he said, forcing his voice to stay calm, his features composed.

"Aren't you the cool one?" Rory snapped, moving into the living room and halting four yards from the chair. "We'll see how high and mighty you act after I'm through with you."

Fred Bullock was propped on his left elbow, perspiration still glistening on his forehead. "If you kill us, Cord, you'll hang."

"Maybe. Maybe not," Rory said. "Do you think I care anymore?"

"We figured you'd left," Fargo remarked.

"I did," Rory said, dripping water into a growing puddle at his feet. "Rebecca talked me into running like a weasel with its tail tucked between its legs. She wanted us to catch up with Lucas and that Whitman girl."

"Why didn't you?" Fargo asked, moving his right hand a fraction of an inch closer to his Colt.

"The reason is simple. I've never run from a fight in my life and I'm not about to start at my age. A man who won't stick up for what's his ain't much of a man in my book."

Bullock cleared his throat. "The smart thing for you to do is hand over that pistol and come along quietly. I promise you'll get a fair trial."

"Trial?" Cord said, and laughed like one driven over the brink of sanity. "You're a jackass, Fred, if you think I'm going to let the law take me alive. After this I'll always be on the run, always have to look over my shoulder, but it will be worth it because I'll have the satisfaction of knowing this son of a bitch is dead!" He jabbed the revolver at Skye.

The marshal started to sit upright.

"No you don't!" Cord barked. "Stay right where you are." He took a stride closer to the chair and glared at Fargo. "I almost did it, you know. My wife and I were over a mile to the east when I thought of you chasing me off my own spread and I got so mad I couldn't hardly see straight."

"Where is your wife?" Fargo asked, his hand creeping nearer to the Colt.

Cord jerked his head toward the front of the house. "Told her to stay outside. What I'm fixing to do to you is no sight for a lady to see."

"You have a nice wife there," Fargo said.

The compliment made Rory recoil in surprise. His eyes narrowed and he snarled, "Not nice enough or she would have done my job for me and cut you down when she caught you poking around our barn. She's like all women. If you don't smack them around now and then they forget how to behave."

An image of Cord bashing his kind wife around brought Fargo's blood to a boil. He almost forgot himself and leaped up.

"Enough palaver!" Cord declared, smirking. "It's time

for me to put an end to the career of the great Trails-man." He raised the revolver until the barrel pointed squarely at Skye's head. "Now I want you to stand. Be sure and keep your hands away from your six-shooter."

To do otherwise invited instant death. Fargo frowned as he stood, his arms out from his sides.

"Good," Cord said. "Now take your left hand, grip your pistol with two fingers, and drop it on the floor."

Again Fargo had no choice but to obey. The Colt smacked down hard on the floor at his feet. "I didn't think you'd shoot me and get this over with," he remarked.

"Hell, no. Not and deprive me of all the fun I aim to have," Cord said, wagging the revolver. "I reckon I'll do to you what Slade did to Reni."

Fargo knew what was coming. Practically everyone west of the Mississippi had heard about the feud between two hard cases named Jack Slade and Jules Reni. Reni had been stealing stock from the company Slade worked for, and when Slade set out to gather proof Reni shot him five times. The locals in Julesburg, Colorado, had expected Slade to die, but he hadn't acquired a reputation as a hard man for nothing. Slade lived, and a year ago had taken his revenge by having Reni tied to a post and then shooting the man to pieces. Only when Reni was on the threshold of dying did Slade walk up, stick his revolver barrel into Reni's mouth, and squeeze the trigger. As an added measure Slade cut off Reni's ears and was still carrying them around as a keepsake he proudly displayed at every saloon he visited.

"Where should I begin?" Cord said, and chortled. He pointed his gun first at Skye's right arm, then at Skye's left leg.

"Rory!" Bullock cried. "Don't!"

"Not another peep out of you, Fred," Cord warned. "I'm saving you for last so you'll have a few more minutes of life. You've always treated me fair and I'm returning the favor. At least your end will be quicklike."

Fargo braced to execute a desperate lunge. He wasn't going to stand there and allow the bastard to shoot him full of holes. Better to go down fighting than to die like a coward.

"I think I'll start with the gut," Cord said, shifting the

barrel so it was trained on Skye's abdomen. His eyes gleaming with anticipation, he extended his arm.

From the doorway a new voice spoke up. "This ain't right, Rory!"

Fargo glanced to his right. Rebecca Cord stood framed in the entrance, her hair and clothes sopping wet, water running down her face and dripping from her chin. Her arms were by her sides, partially hidden by a long slicker she wore.

"What the hell are you doing here, woman?" Cord demanded. "I told you to stay with the horses!"

"This ain't right," Rebecca repeated. "You can't kill these men."

"Go out with the damn horses!"

Rebecca took a step and gazed sadly from Bullock to Skye. "I will not. Rory, I want you to let them go. Come with me now and we'll ride out of here and start over again somewhere else."

Cord's cheeks were tinged with scarlet. "You're trying my patience. Are you out of your mind, talking back to me like this? For the last time, I want you to go mount up and wait for me."

"If you kill a lawman we'll never know a moment's peace." Rebecca stubbornly held her ground. "Think for a minute! You've done more than your share of bad deeds over the years, and I've patiently stood by your side through thick and thin. I never said a word back when you took to robbing folks and leaving them trussed up like you did. And I never complained when we were riding all over Texas stealing cattle. But I draw the line at killing these innocent men."

"Innocent?" Cord roared, and pointed at Fargo. "This Trailsman killed most of our men and drove off the rest. He beat your son and beat me within an inch of my life. I'm fixing to kill him and there isn't a damn thing you can do about it."

"Please," Rebecca said.

Ignoring her, Rory aimed at Fargo's head and thumbed back the hammer. "Since my woman is so squeamish, I reckon I'll make this quick and skedaddle."

"Please," Rebecca said a final time.

Fargo saw Rory sneer and was on the verge of making a bid for the Colt when Rebecca Cord's right arm swept up holding a shotgun. She gripped it in both hands and without hesitation fired, the blast deafening in the confined space, the buckshot ripping into Rory's left side and lifting him clean off his feet to smash against the end of the sofa, then crumple to the floor. Tendrils of acrid gun smoke waved in the air as Fargo scooped up his revolver, but there was no need for any gunplay.

Rory Cord was on his back, his empty hands gesturing feebly, half of his shirt already red with his lifeblood. His eyes were open, flicking back and forth as if seeking something.

The shotgun hit the floor as Rebecca let go and moved with halting steps over to her husband. She knelt, tears pouring down her cheeks to mingle with the raindrops, and took his hand in hers. "I'm sorry," she said hoarsely. "I'm so sorry, Rory. I wish you had listened. I couldn't let you do it."

Cord focused on her. He tried to speak, his lips trembling from the effort. Suddenly he went rigid, gasped loudly, and convulsed before ultimately going limp.

Marshal Bullock had sat up. Grimacing, he managed to stand and shuffled to the Cords. "Thank you, Rebecca."

"He didn't leave me any choice, Fred."

"I know."

"Will you help me bury him? I—I don't quite know if I'm up to it."

Fargo holstered the Colt. "The marshal shouldn't do any hard work for a while. I'll lend a hand if you'll let me."

When Rebecca Cord looked up at him her eyes were filled to the brim with tears. She barely choked out her reply. "Thank you kindly, sir. I'm obliged."

15

The golden sun hovered above the eastern horizon when Skye Fargo rode eastward out of Beartown. He had a full stomach thanks to a delicious meal at Ruth's, where he had learned the doctor was rating Mercia's chances of pulling through as no better than fifty-fifty. The operation had been a success, but Mercia had lost a lot of blood and was extremely weak. Her survival depended on the strength of her will.

He settled his hat more comfortably on his head and avoided one of the many large puddles dotting the rutted dirt track winding like a brown ribbon into the far distance. The storm had raged until four in the morning and the soil was still soaked. All tracks had been obliterated.

Ordinarily, finding Lucas and Marcia would be a difficult task. Rebecca had made the job easier by telling him Rory and Lucas had agreed to meet in a small place called Rock Springs in five days. She'd disclosed the information on one condition; Skye was forced to promise he wouldn't harm Lucas if he could possibly avoid it. Rebecca had revealed other interesting information as well.

Apparently she despised Marcia Whitman. Rebecca regarded Marcia as a hussy who slept with every man she met and who had no business taking up with her son. Marcia had often been out to the ranch for supper, yet not once had she offered to help with the cooking or the dishes. Rebecca felt Marcia's interest in Lucas stemmed from the notion that Lucas would one day inherit the RC. Several times Rebecca tried to convince her son that Marcia was not the right woman for him, but Lucas stubbornly refused to listen.

Skye well remembered the last words Rebecca had spoken to him before he rode from the ranch. "If you go after them, don't take your eyes off that hellcat. She'll kill you as soon as look at you. Mark my words, Mr. Fargo. She's a demon in disguise."

A demon Marcia definitely wasn't, but after what she had done to Mercia he wasn't going to take her lightly. Bullock wanted him to bring her back to Beartown to stand trial and he'd given his word to do his best even though he knew she would resist tooth and nail.

Rock Springs was located approximately one hundred miles from Beartown over rugged, pristine country. He figured on pushing the stallion and completing the journey in two and a half days. Always alert for Indians, he stuck to the rutted track thousands had followed on their way west to Oregon. Mile after mile fell behind him. That night he camped in a grove of trees near a spring.

Day two found him on the move before the sun rose. He was cresting a hill later that morning when before him appeared a wagon train comprised of forty Conestoga wagons. A lean, bearded man who had the air of a seasoned frontiersman rode out to meet him, drawing rein ten feet away.

"Howdy, stranger."

Fargo nodded. "Are you the wagon boss?"

"Yep. The name is Clyborn. Got me a passel of folks headin' for the promised land in Oregon. Who might you be?"

"Skye Fargo."

Clyborn's interest piqued and he studied Skye intently. "Heard of you. What's the trail like ahead?"

"Between here and Beartown it's clear. I didn't see any sign of hostiles."

"Good," the wagon boss said, shifting in his saddle to nod at the wagon train. "To tell you the truth I hope I don't run into any. These pilgrims are farmers, not Indian fighters. Half of them will faint at the first war whoop."

Fargo smiled. "How long ago did you leave Rock Springs?"

"We passed through it four days ago. The damned oxen don't do much better than twelve to fifteen miles a day, if that. I might as well be draggin' an anchor behind my horse."

"See any sign of a man and woman riding by themselves? You wouldn't forget the woman if you did. She's an eyeful with long blond hair."

"Come to think of it, we did. About a day out of Rock Springs, at our noon camp. They rode up and shared some coffee. Seemed to me they were in a bit of a hurry because their horses were ready to keel over. They never did say their names or where they were headin'." Clyborn paused. "You after them?"

Skye nodded.

"Then good hunting," the wagon boss said, and rode back to his charges.

That night Fargo bedded down in a gully and made a fire safe from the high wind. His supper consisted of thick black coffee and salty jerked beef purchased at Nuckoll's General Store prior to his departure. He thought about Mercia, lying close to death because her sister had fallen in love with a no-account and gone completely bad. If Lucas hadn't come along the twins might still be as close as two bumps on a log. Rebecca had claimed Marcia was pure evil compared to her son, but love, as someone had once said, was a two-edged sword. Lucas Cord was no angel.

Chirping birds brought him around the next morning and after more coffee he was on the road again. Toward noon, as he approached a stream, he spied a solitary wagon parked near the water, an enclosed wooden van of the type used by traveling peddlers and patent-medicine men. Sure enough, as he drew closer he read a sign on the side of the van that proclaimed in bold red letters, Doc Black's Remedies For All Ailments. Seated on a log beside a small fire was a wiry man in a black suit and a derby who picked up a rifle as Skye approached, then stood.

"Hello there, my good fellow."

Fargo halted and indicated the wagon. "Are you Doc Black?"

"That I am," the man said proudly. "Are you sickly? I have the cure. Wizard oils, blood pills, cough balsams, stomach bitters, worm destroyers, you name it, old Doc Black has it."

"I'm fine," Fargo said, leaning on his saddle horn. "Did you peddle your wares in Rock Springs?"

"That I did," Black replied. "Had me a run on blood

purifiers like you wouldn't believe. Those ladies who work at the Tower Saloon were in great need of it, I can tell you. Also sold me some squaw vine and mandrake root. Why do you ask?"

"You might have seen a couple I'm looking for, a man in a white hat and a blond woman."

"Why, you must mean the Cords. A lovely pair, if I do say so myself."

"You talked to them?"

Black nodded. "I should say I did. We had adjoining rooms at the Higgins Boardinghouse and ate our meals together a few times. Mrs. Cord is quite nice, but her husband can be rude at times. I tried to sell him some extract of sarsaparilla and he about took my head off. Do you know them well?"

"Better than most," Fargo said. "Thanks." He crossed the stream, splashing water in all directions, and spied the town in the distance. So Lucas and Marcia were posing as man and wife? Or were they married already? He swung to the north. Since the pair would be expecting pursuit from the west and would watch for anyone arriving from that direction, he planned to make a circuit of the town and ride in from the east under cover of darkness.

By late afternoon he was waiting in a stand of trees a mile east of Rock Springs. More jerky satisfied his hunger. When twilight shrouded the land he swung onto the stallion. He saw no one until he was within a quarter of a mile of the town, then three men going in the opposite direction passed him. There were lights on in most of the buildings when he pulled up beside the first one and scanned the single street.

Rock Springs was a smaller version of Beartown. There were two saloons, a store, the boarding house, and several frame homes. A few people were moving about. Otherwise, all was quiet.

Skye checked the cylinder of his Colt to be sure he had bullets in every chamber except the one under the hammer. Then, the revolver resting loosely in its holster, he rode up to the hitch rail in front of the Tower Saloon. Tinny music mingled with gay laughter wafted on the cool air. He strolled to the open door and stood to one side to survey the interior.

At the bar were four men drinking and chatting with a pair of women attired in the kind of dresses only professional ladies of the night would dare wear in public. Four tables were lined up near the left-hand wall. At all four, card games were in progress. Milling idly about were six more men, some watching a game, others talking to women.

His features hardened on spying Lucas Cord seated at the second table, facing away from the entrance. There was no sign of Marcia. He entered, aware of the bartender's scrutiny, and walked forward until he was behind the younger Cord. As there was an empty chair on Cord's right, he asked in a level tone, "Mind if I sit in, gents?"

Lucas froze in the act of discarding. The other two men at the table glanced at him, then at Skye, and pushed their chairs back so they could move swiftly aside should the worse come to pass. "That you, Trailsman?" Lucas asked.

Fargo sat down in the empty chair. "You made good time from Beartown to here."

"Too bad we didn't keep going," Lucas said wistfully, placing his cards on the table. "How did you know we would be here?"

"Your mother told me."

Cord's surprise was evident. "You talked to her? Where was Pa? He'd never allow it."

"Your father is dead," Fargo revealed.

A flush of anger crept up Lucas's face and his right hand drifted toward his unbuttoned jacket. "Did you kill him?" he asked roughly.

"Your mother did."

The two other players exchanged worried looks, stood, and hastened around the table to the bar.

As if transformed to stone, Lucas simply gaped in disbelief at Skye for the better part of a minute. At last he coughed, recovered his composure, and snarled, "You're lying! My ma would never do such a thing."

Fargo didn't bother to argue the issue. There was no point. Lucas would believe what he wanted to believe and nothing else. "She asked me to go easy on you. Not that I want to. But since Bullock can't arrest you for killings done outside of the town limits, I can't take you back for the murder of that cowhand. You're free to do as you please."

"And Marcia?"

"She's wanted for stabbing her sister. I'm taking her back to stand trial."

"I won't let you."

"You can't stop me," Fargo said, and saw fury simmer in Lucas's eyes. Like father, like son, as the saying went. He casually lowered his right hand onto his lap, a palm's width from his Colt.

Cord noted the movement. He slowly twisted in his chair until he was directly facing Skye. "Be reasonable. I love her. I'll protect her with my life if need be."

"That's what it will take if you interfere."

Leaning forward, Lucas lowered his voice, both hands close to his jacket. "I can pay you. My father gave me three thousand dollars to hold until he got here. Every cent is yours if you'll simply ride on out of Rock Springs and leave us in peace." He grinned. "Think of it. Three thousand dollars for not doing a damn thing. You can't make money much easier than that."

Fargo let the loathing he felt inside reflect itself on his face. "You can keep your money, Cord. I agreed to find out what happened to Adam Whitman as a favor to the twins. One thing has led to another, and now I aim to see this business through to the end."

"You're a fool, Trailsman," Lucas said without rancor. "A lot of good men would still be alive today if you hadn't prodded us so hard."

"A man does what he has to do," Fargo said, and bluntly asked the question he still had to answer. "Who killed Adam? You, your father, or one of your hands?"

"What makes you think he's dead?" Lucas rejoined defensively.

"We both know he is," Fargo said, then added, "He loved the twins and his job. He was content living in Beartown. A man like that doesn't just chuck it all and ride off to parts unknown."

"If you ask me, he loved the twins too much."

"Meaning?"

Lucas fidgeted uncomfortably. "Meaning he didn't know when to leave well enough alone. He thought he had the right to tell Marcia how she should live her life, and he didn't. She's a grown woman. She can do as she pleases."

Fargo put two and two together and concluded, "Adam found out about Marcia and you and didn't like it. He wanted her to stop seeing you."

Cord nodded. "We used to meet practically every night in some trees about a mile from Beartown. He got suspicious of her nightly rides and followed her one time."

"Why didn't she tell him at the beginning?"

"Because Whitman hated my pa. They argued one time about the way our hands were acting up in town and Pa shoved Whitman around a little. From then on Whitman went out of his way to cause trouble for us. He wrote editorials in his paper saying we didn't know how to live in a civilized community, as he put it. And there was more, much more, a lot of it just name-calling. He got away with it because he was a journalist. If anyone else had treated us that way, Pa wouldn't have stood for it."

"Did your father know about Marcia and you?"

Again Cord nodded. "He didn't understand what I saw in her, but he gave me his blessing. Ma never did take to her."

"What finally happened to Adam?"

Lucas straightened and leaned back. "I reckon I've talked enough, probably more than I should." He paused. "For the last time, Fargo, I want you to leave us alone. Ride back to Beartown and tell that fat marshal you couldn't find us."

"I can't do that."

"Damn you all to hell," Lucas said calmly, and his right hand suddenly whipped under his coat and came out holding a derringer.

Skye was prepared. Even as Cord's hand vanished under the coat he was rising, his left hand under the table, his powerful shoulder muscles uncoiling as he lifted the table and heaved, throwing it into Lucas who staggered backward, tripped, and fell against a man from the first table who was in the act of standing. Both men and a chair went down. Lucas struggled to untangle himself, and in that moment Skye took two swift steps, clenched his right fist, and slammed Lucas full on the mouth.

Cord's head snapped back, blood spurted from his crushed lips. He sagged and the derringer clattered on the floor.

Taking a stride backward, Fargo waited.

Lucas shook his head, rubbed his chin, and glowered. "This makes twice you've walloped me," he spat, his words distorted, blood trickling from both corners of his mouth. "There won't be a third time." Hissing angrily, he came up off the floor in a rush.

Fargo nimbly sidestepped and in the bargain planted his right fist in Cord's stomach. Lucas doubled over, gurgling. A left jab sent him tottering into the wall.

"Here now!" the bartender was bellowing. "I won't have fighting in my place! Take your dispute outside!"

"I'm going after Marcia," Fargo told Cord. "If you're smart you won't try to stop me." He started to pivot, keeping one eye on Lucas, and it was well he did.

Uttering a strangled cry of sheer rage, Lucas Cord clawed at the six-shooter on his right hip, his hand a blur. His features betrayed his state of mind. He thirsted for the death of this big man in buckskins who had caused the ruin of his family's fledgling cattle empire. He wanted to see his slugs rip into Fargo's body and have the satisfaction of gloating over Fargo's bullet-riddled corpse. But his right hand was not quite clear of the holster when an intense burning sensation speared through his chest and his ears rang to the boom of a revolver. He was rocked on his heels but stayed upright. Frantically he tried once more to draw. This time there were two shots. He vaguely felt something smash into his forehead and then he was falling forward in an immense black tunnel.

Fargo held the Colt steady as Cord slammed onto the floor. He nudged the body with his boot, then turned. All eyes were on him, a few displaying fear, most frankly curious. The bartender was clearly mad. "You all saw it. He pulled a hideout on me," he said.

"You'd better light out, mister," said a man at the last table. "That there was Lucas Cord. His pa owns a big spread over near Beartown. He'll come gunning for you with all of his hands."

"Rory Cord and most of his men are dead," Fargo disclosed.

A few men shared skeptical looks. "How do you know?" one asked.

"I killed them."

The ensuing silence was thick enough to cut with a butter knife. No one seemed inclined to express any doubts about Skye's statement, and the men between him and the door abruptly decided they wanted to stand closer to the bar.

At last the bartender spoke. "Who might you be, stranger?"

"Skye Fargo."

"Heard of you," the bartender said, and gazed at Lucas Cord. "Did you have to go and shoot him in the head? Now he'll bleed out all over the place."

"He didn't leave me much choice," Fargo responded. He stepped to the door, then paused. "A blond woman came into Rock Springs with him. She's wanted in Beartown for stabbing her sister. Anyone seen her around?"

A grizzled old-timer nodded. "I saw her in front of the boarding house an hour or so ago."

"Cord and her have a room there," confirmed a woman in a red dress.

Fargo replaced the spent rounds in the Colt, slid the gun into his holster, and strolled out into the brisk night. People drawn by the shots were moving toward the saloon, a half dozen almost to the entrance. They halted on seeing him.

"What happened in there?" one asked.

"Someone bit off more than he could chew," Fargo answered, and made for the Higgins Boardinghouse which lay across the street and several buildings down. He watched the front windows, half expecting Marcia to be peering out since she must have heard the shots. But he reached the boardwalk without being spotted just as a thin man wearing spectacles stepped outside.

"Howdy, mister. Do you want a room?" the man asked absently while staring at the Tower Saloon. "My name is Pritchet. I'm the clerk."

"I'm looking for a woman who goes by the name of Marcia Cord. Which room is she in?"

The man adjusted his glasses on his nose before replying in a cold tone, "Mrs. Cord is a married lady. Perhaps you should wait for her husband to get back before you go up to see her."

"Her husband is dead. So which room?"

Pritchet gaped, then glanced from Skye to the saloon. "Oh, my!" he exclaimed. "I'm not supposed to give out room numbers to every saddle tramp who comes through town, and if you had anything to do with her husband's death I'm certainly not going to allow you to—"

Fargo's patience had worn thin. If he didn't find Marcia soon she might get away. He grabbed the clerk by the front of the shirt, cutting off the rest of whatever the man was fixing to say, and hauled him off his feet. "Friend, I don't have time for this. Marcia Cord tried to kill her own sister a few days ago in Beartown so don't tell me how much of a lady she is. All I want is her room number. Now!"

"Room seven!" Pritchet blurted. "Take a right at the top of the stairs."

"Much obliged," Fargo said, lowering the frightened clerk to the boardwalk. Inside was a small lobby with a counter to the right and stairs to the left. As he moved toward the latter he gazed down a narrow hallway and spotted a back door hanging wide open. Concerned, he quickly climbed to the second floor and saw the door to the Cords' room also open. A hasty check verified his hunch.

Marcia Whitman was gone.

16

A bald man in dirty overalls was brushing down a brown mare under a lantern in the stable when Fargo rode up to the entrance. "Are you the owner?" he inquired.

"Sure am," the man said while brushing briskly. "Evans is the name. Something you want?"

"Did Lucas and Marcia Cord rent stalls from you?"

The man stopped and regarded Skye quizzically. "They did. The man's horse is still here. The wife took her mare out a few minutes ago. She was in some sort of a hurry, I can tell you. Never saw a woman saddle up so fast in all my life."

"Did you see which way she went?"

"No, sir. I couldn't. She rode straight behind the livery, which I thought was strange. I never did hear any hoofbeats after that."

"Thanks," Fargo said, and wheeled the Ovaro eastward. Marcia was a shrewd one. She must have seen him as he came out of the saloon and promptly fled out the back door of the hotel. After obtaining her mare she had ridden behind the livery to avoid using the main street, and by holding her mount to a show walk until she was out of town she had prevented the liveryman from determining which direction she had taken. But it had to be east. To the north and south extended hundreds of square miles of harsh wilderness. To the west was Beartown, where Marshal Bullock would arrest her on sight.

He galloped out of town, passing a crowd gathered in front of the Tower Saloon. Pritchet was among them. The clerk and about fifteen other men watched him depart with fire in their eyes. If nothing else he would be the talk of Rock Springs for the next week or two.

The rutted road, such as it was, wound among hills and canyons. After a mile and a half he stopped to listen but heard only the wind sighing through nearby trees. Marcia must be a mile or better in front of him but her mare was no match for the pinto. He would catch her before midnight.

An hour later Fargo saw a single wagon coming in the opposite direction. He reined up to give the stallion a brief respite until the wagon reached them. In the driver's seat was a rangy man in homespun clothes. "Hello," Fargo greeted him.

"Whoa, there!" the driver shouted to his mules, and yanked on the ribbons as he applied the brake. He spat a wad of tobacco out of the corner of his mouth, then cocked an eye at Skye. "Howdy yourself, mister. You need something?"

"A blond woman passed you a while ago. How far back was it?"

The man chuckled. "I wish to hell a woman had passed me. It would have helped to take my mind off the hard day I've had." He chuckled louder. "Have you been hittin' the bottle, stranger?"

"A woman didn't pass you?"

"Sure didn't. What's she doing ridin' by herself so far from town at this time of night anyway? Doesn't she know there might be Injuns or outlaws around?"

Fargo was stumped. Had Marcia seen the wagon coming and hid beside the trail until it had gone by? Or was it possible she hadn't headed east after all?

"I've been on the road for days, myself," the man disclosed. "Hauling freight to Rock Springs and Beartown. Everything was fine until yesterday morning. Then one of the wheels got busted." He spat more tobacco. "Have you ever tried to fix a broken wheel out in the middle of nowhere? I was fit to be tied."

Think! Fargo goaded himself. He must try and put himself in Marcia's shoes in order to figure out where she had gone. Due east was the logical choice, but what if she had decided to pick another way since she knew he would give chase and she wanted to lose him above all else? What was the best way to do that? Hide in Rock Springs? No, because he would be back there once he realized she had not headed east. Make camp in the wild? Possibly, but he doubted it. There hadn't been time for her to buy supplies before leaving town.

"Are you all right, mister?" the driver asked.

"Fine," Fargo said. "Thanks for the help." Touching his spurs to the Ovaro, he rode on. For the time being he would act on the assumption Marcia had steered clear of the freighter. If, however, he failed to overtake her by midnight, he would catch a few hours shut-eye and examine the trail closely in the morning. If there were no fresh tracks he would turn around and check for sign all the way back to Rock Springs. Eventually he would find her.

Like all experienced frontiersmen, Skye could tell the approximate time by the positions of various stars and constellations. So, hours later, when the alignment of the Big Dipper told him that it was close to the witching hour, he stopped in a small clearing beside the trail and stripped his saddle and bedroll off the stallion. Since it was so late he dispensed with a fire and made a cold camp instead. Picketing the Ovaro took a minute, and then he spread out his ground sheet and blankets and turned in, lying on his back and pondering the series of events since that fateful day when he came to the aid of the twins. Marcia certainly had fooled him, as she had everyone else. No one had suspected her link to Lucas Cord except for her father, who shortly thereafter was missing. A disturbing possibility occurred to him and he hoped he was wrong.

He closed his eyes, idly listening to the crunch of the pinto's teeth as the stallion grazed. The breeze stirred a nearby thicket. Lulled into drowsiness, he started to doze when the crunching suddenly stopped and the Ovaro nickered lightly. Instantly he raised his head to survey their surroundings. The pinto was gazing to the northwest so something must be out there. An animal perhaps, a mountain lion or a bear. Or Indians.

Skye reached under the blanket and gripped his Colt. Nothing unusual happened, and he was lowering his head when the dull thud of approaching hoofs brought him to his feet in a rush, the Colt leveled and cocked. He spied a riderless horse moving toward the Ovaro and moved to intercept. Not until the animal was ten feet off did he recognize the mount as Marcia's. He quickly grabbed the reins.

The mare was lathered with sweat and breathing heavily. Clearly Marcia had come close to riding the horse into the ground. Its head drooped and it snorted loudly.

Fargo was puzzled. What had the mare been doing northwest of his camp? There was only one explanation he could think of, namely that Marcia must have stopped for the night somewhere in the vicinity before he arrived, then the mare had picked up the stallion's scent and decided to make a social call. But the explanation didn't hold water because Marcia's saddle and bedroll were still on her horse. He absently placed his left hand on the seat, feeling the warmth of the leather on his palm. A saddle that warm could only mean one thing: Marcia had just dismounted.

With a start he realized he had been duped and launched into a dive at the very moment a revolver cracked in the brush. A brief, searing pain lanced his temple and then he was on his stomach, dazed, his arms outspread. He lay still, gathering his wits, certain he had only been creased. There was another reason not to move. Marcia must be somewhere close at hand, watching him, ready to fire again if he so much as lifted a finger. So he imitated a log and waited for her next move.

Again he marveled at her cleverness. She must have pulled off the trail and waited for him to pass, then shadowed him until he camped. Because he'd been concentrating on the trail ahead and not to the rear, he'd never caught on. She'd waited until she thought he was asleep, then she had sent her mare in as a ruse to get him on his feet where she would have a perfect target sluggish from being so abruptly awakened. He had to hand it to her. She would make a damn fine Apache.

Stealthy footfalls sounded. He still had the Colt in his right hand and could roll and fire if he heard her cock her weapon, which she might do if she decided to put a few more slugs into him to be sure he was dead. The footsteps drew closer until a wicked laugh let him know she was next to his left elbow.

"So much for the great Trailsman! You weren't so tough! It's a pity I didn't do this days ago."

Skye cracked his eyelids. She stood inches from his arm, her pistol in her right hand. Instead of a dress she now wore jeans, a black jacket, and short boots.

"You spoiled everything, you bastard!" Marcia said sourly. "In a few years the Cords would have become rich and would have owned the biggest ranch in the whole territory. Lucas would be powerful and influential, with me right by his side sharing his wealth and power." She cursed. "Now all my plans are up in smoke because of you!"

He nearly cried out when she unexpectedly kicked him in the side. Holding himself still, he allowed the pain to subside before making his move.

"All that I did was for nothing," Marcia lamented. "The Cords have been ruined, the man I was going to marry is dead, and I'm left—."

Fargo lashed out with the speed of a striking sidewinder, sweeping his left arm into Marcia's shins with all of his strength. She uttered a startled yelp as she crashed down onto her elbows and knees. Before she could recover, Fargo was on his feet and bending down to snatch the pistol from her fingers, his Colt pointed at her head. He had listened to her ramble on long enough. She was the key to understanding everything that had happened and the only way to get straight answers was by questioning her. "We meet again," he said dryly.

"Damn you!" Marcia growled, rising to her knees and rubbing her right arm. In the moonlight her face was a pale mask of implacable hatred.

"It's nice to see you, too," Fargo said.

"I know you killed Lucas," said Marcia. "I was riding past the back of the saloon when a man out front yelled to someone else about how you shot him." She frowned. "Not that I was surprised. I heard the gunfire and saw you come out of Tower's place."

"He drew first."

Marcia's lips twitched. "There's one consolation for me. His father will hunt you down to the ends of the earth. You won't have anywhere to hide."

Skye wedged her revolver under his belt and said, "There are a few things you should know. For one thing, Rory Cord is dead, shot down by Rebecca. For another, your sister is still alive. At least she was when I left Beartown."

"Mercia alive?" Marcia said, shocked at the news.

"Why did you do it?" Fargo asked. "Why did you stab her?"

"Why else? She was fixing to put out a special edition about the Cords being rustlers. I couldn't allow that. I was going to burn the house down, too, but you showed up." Marcia rested her hands on her thighs. "Rory and Lucas needed time to sell their spread so we'd have money to start new lives elsewhere. If the news about their rustling days became common knowledge they wouldn't have been able to sell a single calf."

"So you tried to take the life of your own sister, your twin no less," Fargo said in disgust.

"I would do anything to protect Lucas. I loved him."

"Is that why you slept with me? To find out how much I had learned about the Cords?"

"Of course," Marcia responded. "I wanted to warn Lucas if you came too close to the truth."

"You knew about the rustling?"

"Lucas didn't keep any secrets from me. No matter what you might have thought of him, he always treated me with respect. If all had gone well, if we had been able to bury his past and increase the RC herd like his father wanted, he would have set me up in a fine house and we would have lived in grand style."

Fargo relaxed slightly and let the barrel of his Colt sag. "Why did you keep your romance a secret right from the start? Why didn't you come right out and tell your father?"

"Don't you know? My father hated Rory Cord. And my father could be a tyrant when he wanted to be. No daughter of his would be permitted to take up with the son of a sworn enemy. So I kept it a secret and saw Lucas on the sly," Marcia said, her right hand straying to her hip. "I never expected my father to stoop so low as to spy on me."

"Is that why you killed him? Because he wanted you to stop seeing Lucas?"

Marcia's right hand slid off her hip to her boot. "That was part of it," she said with no evidence of remorse. "Pa found out about the cattle. Probably by examining the brands." She bowed her head. "He'd forbidden me to go meet Lucas but I couldn't help myself. I snuck off one evening and he trailed me again. This time he made a scene, riding up and ordering Lucas to leave me alone. When Lucas refused, Pa said he would fix the Cords for good. He said he was going right back to town and tell the marshal about the cattle." She paused and sighed. "I couldn't let that happen."

"What did you do?"

"This," Marcia said, and came off the ground in a rush, the moonlight glinting off the blade of a slender knife, her features contorted in feral blood lust. She swung savagely, aiming at Skye's midsection.

The attack took Fargo completely unawares. He stumbled backward, trying to level the Colt to cover her, and tripped over a bush. As he went down she swung again, the blade striking the Colt, batting the gun aside. Marcia pounced, lifting her right arm high to plunge the knife into his chest but her boots struck his, causing her to trip and throwing her off balance. She came down to the right of him instead of on top of him. Fargo rolled in the opposite direction and surged erect, his finger on the trigger.

Marcia was flat on her stomach, her disheveled hair covering her face.

"Nice try," Skye said. He stayed well out of reach. Her arms were underneath her chest and she might jump up and swing at any instant. "Now stand up and drop that knife."

Marcia didn't move.

"Did you hear me?" Skye asked.

There was no reply.

Moving cautiously, wary of a trick, Skye edged nearer, gripped her by the shoulder, and flipped her over. The knife hilt jutted from Marcia's chest, ringed by a dark stain spreading rapidly over her blouse. Her lovely eyes were wide open but blank. He felt for a pulse, found none, and stood.

Marcia Whitman had been deceitful to the last, allowing him to question her while all the time she was working her hand closer to the knife. She had been a natural born killer, as deadly as any man he ever met, a schemer and manipulator who eliminated anyone who got in her way. Now that she was gone he could think of only one thing to say, and said it.

"Good riddance."

                              *   *   *

"The doc says you'll be as good as new in two weeks
or so," Fargo commented.

Lying on the bed in her room, Mercia looked up at
him and managed a wan smile. "I can hardly wait. The
past week has been unbearable what with having nothing
to do but lie here and think about her."

"She took the wrong path. She paid the price."

"Is that all there was to it?" Mercia responded. "I
wonder. She always was headstrong but I never suspected
she would go as far as she did. And I thought I knew her!
How can one person be so utterly wrong about another?"

"We all make mistakes."

"But she was my own sister! We shared everything
since we were children. We were as close as two people
can be. Yet now I find out we were completely different."

Fargo shifted in his chair. "Some folks don't show their
true colors until they're crossed. They're a lot like mountain lions. Leave them alone and they'll go their own
way in peace. Rile them and they come at you with their
claws flashing."

"I suppose," Mercia said uncertainly, then gazed into
his eyes. "Thanks again for everything."

"I wish it could have turned out differently," Fargo
said. He stood, gave her a kiss on the cheek, and stepped
to the door. "Ruth will be back in a couple of hours to
check your bandages. She said to tell you she'll bring
along some more chicken soup."

Mercia grinned. "I already have it coming out my ears.
She swears by it when someone isn't feeling well."

"Want me to sneak a steak to you?" Fargo asked, and
was rewarded with the first hearty laughter from her lips
since she had been stabbed.

"You'd better not. Ruth would have a fit," Mercia
said, then became serious. "If you're ever back this way
will you stop by?"

"We're friends, aren't we?" Fargo replied, about to
leave when he remembered something. "Oh. There's a
Captain Vogel out front. He rode into town with an army
patrol this morning. Claims to know you and wants to
come on up."

"Jess Vogel?" Mercia said, brightening. "Yes, he used

to stop by the *Chronicle* office whenever he was in town. I'd like to see him very much."

"I'll tell him," Skye said, and winked. "Just behave yourself."

"Always," Mercia declared. "What about you? Where are you headed now?"

"Wherever the wind blows me."

LOOKING FORWARD!

**The following is the opening
section from the next novel in the exciting
Trailsman series from Signet:**

THE TRAILSMAN #132
KENTUCKY COLTS

*Kentucky, 1860, where the Wabash
joins the Ohio, a land that
wore respectability as a mask
that hid hate, greed,
twisted love and death . . .*

"You've your nerve."

"That's been said before."

"My husband's the mayor of this town."

"Hell, I know that. He sent for me."

"Then how dare you say those things to me?"

"You've been wanting me to say them, honey. You've been sending signals ever since I got here three days ago."

"You've misunderstood simple politeness."

"I'm called the Trailsman, remember? I read signs. That's my life, reading signs."

"I'm hardly a blade of grass or some prairie trail."

"A sign's a sign, a trail's a trail, grass or ass, prairie or pussy. There's not much difference."

"When the mayor gets back I'm going to tell him what you said to me and he'll send you packing."

"No, you won't and no, he won't."

"What makes you so sure I won't?"

"I told you, I read signs. I know teasin' from thirstin' I can tell playin' from pantin'."

"I don't have to wait for my husband to get back. When he's away I'm the acting mayor. I can have you thrown out of town right now."

"On what charge?"

"I'll think of something. Disorderly conduct. That'll do."

"Honey, I haven't started being disorderly."

The big man with the handsomely chiseled face stepped back, but his lake-blue eyes stayed on the woman in front of him. Libby Bradbury was still on the sunny side of forty, about five feet, five inches tall with a slightly overdone, earthy body she emphasized with tight outfits and low-cut necklines that showed the cleavage of deep breasts. Blond hair that kept its blondness with the help of a bottle just avoided looking brassy. Worn short, it framed a compact face, still attractive with enough roundness to it to push away the tiny wrinkles of time. Full hips, a small nose, and dark brown eyes that seemed to hold a perpetual smolder completed the picture.

"You leave this house at once, Mr. Fargo," Libby Bradbury said, drawing indignation around her.

"Just what I was going to do," Skye Fargo said. "But I'll be back tomorrow night. I'm feeling kindly."

"Kindly?"

"Yes. I'll give you one more chance to do what you want to do."

"You'll be wasting your time," she snapped.

"Tell me not to come," he challenged and saw her eyes grow smaller, her tongue slide across her full lips for an instant. Then she lifted her chin and met the mocking smile in his eyes with bold defiance.

"Don't come," she said, and he shrugged and started to turn to the front door of the house. "Are you convinced now?" she tossed at him.

"Are you?" he laughed as he pulled the door open and stepped outside into the night. The woman came to the doorway and watched him pull himself into the saddle, and he saw the light from inside the house outline the curves of her full-hipped figure. Her voice came to him, her tone carefully correct and aloof.

"Of course, you can come by tomorrow night to see if the mayor's come back," she said. "That'd be different."

He let his smile answer, and she spun on her heel and slammed the door shut. The smile stayed with him as he put the magnificent Ovaro into a slow walk through the dark streets of the town. Libby Bradbury had been only one of the surprises he'd had since arriving in town. But she certainly had been the pleasantest and most intriguing. She had tossed a lot of questions at him when he'd arrived to see Sam Bradbury, none of which he could answer, and he'd first thought her signals had been just window-dressing to get answers. But he had seen that tried often enough, and he knew the difference. Libby Bradbury was both actively curious and actively smoldering.

The town itself had been another surprise. It was much more respectable than he's expected, with a bank, a hotel, a proper meeting hall, a number of white-fenced homes, and a thorough assortment of shops from a barber to a blacksmith. But he realized he shouldn't have expected a frontier town. This part of Kentucky where it bordered on Missouri was no longer what it had been when Daniel Boone, John Sevier, and Jim Robertson opened the land. Few families came down Boone's Trace any longer, and the old Kentucky cabins with their Piedmont heritage were hardly seen anymore, nor were the old splint brooms and home wool cards for weaving. Men no longer staked their claims by marking "witness trees" with ax marks. Land was registered properly now.

Yet that had all been less than seventy years back, and while most of the big game was gone, Kentucky was still a rich and fertile land. While the old wild farms had given way to proper plantation farming and horse-breeding land, its heritage was still in the land and its people. Respectability wasn't ever much of a thick cloak and in places here it was but a thin veneer. Yet it didn't seem the kind of town or land that would need the talents of a Trailsman, and Fargo still wondered about the note that had brought him here as he walked the Ovaro down the dark night streets toward the yellow glow of light a little past the center of town. The sounds of voices, laughter, and the clinking of glasses drifted into the night as he reached the saloon, dismounted, and tethered the horse at the hitching post.

The somewhat elegant name of the town—Windsor Bell—had been echoed in the sign over the swinging doors to the saloon. *Bell's Belles,* it proclaimed in faded gold lettering, and he pushed his way through the doors. This made his third night's visit to the saloon since he'd arrived, but he was still very much a stranger and regarded as such by the regulars. The long bar took up one side of the room, tables along the other, and girls in black stockings and abbreviated outfits tended to the customers, all of them with faces too cynical too soon. Perhaps the town was respectable, but the saloon was little different than any other anywhere. One end of the bar was relatively uncrowded, and he stepped to the wooden rail.

"Bourbon," he said. "No bar slop, please." The bartender brought a bottle from under the counter and set it in front of him with a shot glass. Fargo started to reach for the bottle when two men stepped to the bar, one on either side of him, and suddenly he felt others pressing up behind him. He started to turn when he felt the Colt jerked from his holster. He spun to see three men back away, one stuffing the Colt into his pocket. The two men at each side also stepped back, and Fargo's eyes narrowed at the man who'd taken his Colt, a tall but thin figure with an unkempt mustache. "I'd give that back, mister," Fargo growled.

"You can have it after we see you out of town," the man said. "We don't want anybody gettin' shot."

"You're not seeing anybody out of town, either, so give it back," Fargo said. The man wore a loose calfskin jacket over the top part of his thin frame, and the Colt made a bulge in his pocket.

"Just come along and there'll be no trouble," the man said. Fargo's eyes swept the other four. All ordinary cowhand types, one in a tan Stetson showing his nervousness.

But he wasn't about to let them have their way in some isolated spot.

"Wrong again. There's going to be trouble," Fargo said.

The thin one muttered out of the side of his mouth to the others. "Get him," he said, and they started forward. Fargo's hand shot out, closed around the bottle on the bar, and he swung it in a backhand sweep, felt it smash against the side of a face.

"Oh, Jesus," a voice cried out as Fargo turned, saw the man fall backward, one hand clutched to the side of his head. The others had paused for a moment but now came at him again. Fargo, clutching the neck of the broken bottle in his hand, ducked a swinging right and brought the jagged bottle upward. The sharp glass sliced into the armpit of one of his attackers, and the man screamed in pain as he twisted and fell stumbling away.

"Get the sheriff and the mayor," Fargo heard the bartender call out as he twisted away from the three figures that rushed at him. As the screams of the girls filled the background, he turned and glimpsed one of the three leap at him from the rear and braced himself as the man landed on his back. Throwing the piece of bottle away to avoid falling on it, he let himself go forward, dropped to his knees, and tossed the man over his head. He dived to one side as a kick missed his head, then rolled across the floor to come up at a table. He came to his knees, saw four of the five figures charging at him, the one with the side of his face streaming red.

Fargo half rose, spun, and upended the round table as the thin figure and another man reached him. He used the table as a battering ram, putting all the strength of his leg muscles behind it as he smashed it into the two men. They went backward as he pushed and one stumbled, went to one knee. Fargo rose from behind the table swinging a long, looping left that had lost a little of its power when he caught the tall, thin one on the point of the jaw. The man staggered backward and dropped to one knee, and Fargo saw the one with the bloodstained face diving at him across the table, his arms outstretched, his mouth twisted in fury and pain. Fargo stepped back and pulled the table with him and the man fell forward off balance. Fargo's left hook and following right landed flush on his jaw, and he flew backward, twisting in a half circle before he hit the floor.

The other two came around the table and charged at him, arms swinging blows. They were bumping into each other in their rush to get at him, and Fargo sidestepped, sank a hard left into the nearest one's midsection. The man grunted as he doubled up. The other one shifted, rushed again, and Fargo ducked his wild, roundhouse blows, lifted a tremendous uppercut that landed with all the strength of his upper arm behind it. The man almost jackknifed backward as he flew through the air and landed on the floor. The other had regained enough breath to attack again, but Fargo easily blocked his amateurish blows, ducked under a particularly wild swing, seized his arm, twisted and flung the man halfway across the room. His somewhat paunchy figure slammed into the bar, where he hung for a moment and then slithered to the floor to lay half against the brass footrest.

Fargo spun as he heard a sound just to his right and saw that the thin one had recovered enough to try again. He ducked away from a downward punch, blocked a follow-through left, and sank his own right deep into the man's abdomen. As the thin figure doubled over, Fargo brought his knee up hard into the man's face. The man's head snapped back as he sailed through the air and landed spread-eagled on the floor.

Fargo drew himself erect and scanned the scene. His five assailants were unconscious in various positions spread across the barroom floor, almost from one side to the other, ending with the paunchy figure lying against the base of the bar. The girls and a number of the customers were crowded against the walls, looking on now in awed silence.

Fargo stepped to the thin man and retrieved his Colt just as Libby Bradbury strode in with a slightly built, gray-haired man with a tired face and a sheriff's badge attached to his shirt. Libby Bradbury wore an outer coat wrapped around herself, and she halted to stare wide-eyed at the scene. She looked up as Fargo paused beside her. "Now, that's disorderly conduct, honey," he said as he walked from the bar.

Outside, he swung onto the Ovaro and rode slowly away from the saloon. The attack had been just one more thing in what was becoming a list of surprises. He rode the pinto up into the low hills, found a stand of honey locust, and made a small fire to warm up some of the beef jerky from his saddlebag. When he finished eating, he sat back and let the fire burn itself out as his thoughts turned backward, first to the letter that had brought him to Windsor Bell and then to but a few days ago when he'd neared the town.

CANYON O'GRADY RIDES ON

☐ **CANYON O'GRADY #9: COUNTERFEIT MADAM** by Jon Sharpe
(167252—$3.50)

☐ **CANYON O'GRADY #10: GREAT LAND SWINDLE** by Jon Sharpe
(168011—$3.50)

☐ **CANYON O'GRADY #11: SOLDIER'S SONG** by Jon Sharpe
(168798—$3.50)

☐ **CANYON O'GRADY #12: RAILROAD RENEGADES** by Jon Sharpe
(169212—$3.50)

☐ **CANYON O'GRADY #13: ASSASSIN'S TRAIL** by Jon Sharpe
(169646—$3.50)

☐ **CANYON O'GRADY #15: DEATH RANCH** by Jon Sharpe
(170490—$3.50)

☐ **CANYON O'GRADY #16: BLOOD AND GOLD** by Jon Sharpe
(170946—$3.50)

☐ **CANYON O'GRADY #17: THE KILLERS' CLUB** by Jon Sharpe
(171314—$3.50)

☐ **CANYON O'GRADY #18: BLOOD BOUNTY** by Jon Sharpe
(171985—$3.50)

☐ **CANYON O'GRADY #19: RIO GRANDE RANSOM** by Jon Sharpe
(172396—$3.50)

☐ **CANYON O'GRADY #20: CALIFORNIA VENGEANCE** by Jon Sharpe
(173058—$3.50)

Buy them at your local bookstore or use this convenient coupon for ordering.

NEW AMERICAN LIBRARY
P.O. Box 999, Bergenfield, New Jersey 07621

Please send me the books I have checked above.
I am enclosing $_____ (please add $2.00 to cover postage and handling).
Send check or money order (no cash or C.O.D.'s) or charge by Mastercard or
VISA (with a $15.00 minimum). Prices and numbers are subject to change without
notice.

Card #_____ Exp. Date _____
Signature_____
Name_____
Address_____
City _____ State _____ Zip Code _____
For faster service when ordering by credit card call **1-800-253-6476**
Allow a minimum of 4-6 weeks for delivery. This offer is subject to change without notice.

There's an epidemic with 27 million victims. And no visible symptoms.

It's an epidemic of people who can't read.

Believe it or not, 27 million Americans are functionally illiterate, about one adult in five.

The solution to this problem is you... when you join the fight against illiteracy. So call the Coalition for Literacy at toll-free 1-800-228-8813 and volunteer.

Volunteer Against Illiteracy. The only degree you need is a degree of caring.